# An Oxford Tragedy

# An Oxford Tragedy

by

## J. C. Masterman

Dover Publications, Inc., New York

This Dover edition, first published in 1981, is an unabridged republication of the work originally published by
Victor Gollancz, London, in 1933.

*International Standard Book Number: 0-486-24165-3*
*Library of Congress Catalog Card Number: 81-66298*

Manufactured in the United States of America
Dover Publications, Inc.
180 Varick Street
New York, N.Y. 10014

*A quelli il popolo,*
*Che teme un morso,*
*Fa largo, e subito*
*Muta discorso:*
*A noi repubblica*
*Di lieto umore,*
*Tutti spalancano*
*Le braccia e il core!*
*A conti fatti*
*Beati i matti!*

GIUSTI:
*Le Memorie di Pisa*

# CHAPTER ONE

IF you open the Oxford University *Calendar* and turn to
St Thomas's College you will find my name – Francis
Wheatley Winn, Vice-President and Senior Tutor. A note
at the bottom of the page will make it clear to the initiated
that I won, in my youth, some academic distinction, and
that I take my part in the administrative side of University
life. That is all that the *Calendar* will reveal, but for the
purpose of this history, I must say something more, for, in
the nature of things, you must see it all through my eyes,
or rather – to be more exact – through my spectacles.
And there at once, before we are fairly started, is a difficulty. For you must see it through those spectacles or not at
all, and they, no doubt, are a little blurred with prejudices
and misty with my old-fashioned sentimentality. I have
taught history all my life, and, though I have written no
book, I have sought patiently enough for the truth. I
should like to think now that I could set down all this
story objectively – without a hint of my own personality
or my own feelings – but I know that to be impossible, and I
shall not even attempt to do it. No, if I am to tell the whole
truth it can only be the truth as I saw it, and you, for your
part, must resign yourself to seeing it through spectacles
which you can neither polish nor remove.

I am a don; my age is sixty; I flatter myself that I am
broad-minded, and that I have intelligence above the
average; I surmise that by habit of mind I am critical rather
than constructive. Sometimes in moments of self-examina-
tion I admit that I am apt to be a little fussy and ineffective.
To myself, I confess, I am a subject of profound interest:
the examination of my own mental processes is a never-
failing source of pleasure to me, and I like, in moments of
leisure, to let my fancy construct for me the life which I

might have lived had I plunged into the world of politics or letters, or challenged comparison with my intellectual equals at the Bar. I live in imagination a series of lives of honourable distinction, encouraged by public recognition and applauded by the great world. But only in imagination. In sober fact, since I took my degree, I have never seriously considered deserting the security which my fellowship gives me. For the truth is that I am donnish, and my life is bound up in the life of the college to which I belong.

I must not describe my own character in too much detail. A searching analysis of it would indeed be of absorbing interest to myself, but I have enough judgement to know that it would be intolerable for those of you who read these pages. I am a middle-aged don with a tendency to introspection and absurdly careful of my own reputation; we will leave it at that. Let me give up speaking of myself, and tell instead a plain tale of all that happened that evening – the evening of which we still speak as the night of the murder. Perhaps in the telling, my own character will become clearer than if I spent a chapter in the describing of it; perhaps even it will become a little clearer than I could wish.

It was only about seven o'clock, then, as I crossed the Quad, but I had dressed early, for I had two duties to discharge before dinner that night. In the first place, I wanted a few words with Maurice Hargreaves, our Dean, about an undergraduate in whom I was interested. Scarborough was the son of an old friend and early pupil of mine at Oxford, and had been accordingly commended to my special care. He was not himself my pupil, for the combined influence of his father and of the Headmaster of the very expensive public school which he had adorned had succeeded in urging him, not very willingly, into the further study of the classics, whilst I profess modern history; I had, however, endeavoured, in the optimistic though

8

rather muddled phrase of Fred Scarborough, 'to give the boy a leg up, and keep an eye on him.' The effect had not so far been noticeably successful. Scarborough was now still only in his second term, but he had already acquired something of a reputation for idleness and as a rebel against authority. With my knowledge of Fred's own character as a young man to guide me I had interpreted my instruction in a liberal spirit, and the eye which I had kept upon him had been not infrequently an intentionally blind one, but I was beginning to feel that the time was rapidly approaching when I must make some effort to check some of my protégé's extravagances. That he had already, in his first term, run foul of his tutor, Shirley, had neither impressed nor alarmed me, for Shirley had the unfortunate habit of alienating the sympathy and acquiring the dislike of almost all those with whom he came in contact. A brilliant scholar, he was constitutionally incapable of curing his sarcastic and biting tongue, and his colleagues and pupils alike winced under a contempt of speech and manner which he seemed to make little or no attempt to mollify or conceal. Never in his life had Shirley suffered a fool gladly; and even his acquaintances who could claim some intellectual eminence were fortunate if they did not harbour in their minds the memory of caustic and even humiliating corrections from him. That Scarborough, who was the essence of high-spirited and good-natured mediocrity, should resent the ill-concealed contempt of his tutor was only to be expected, and caused me no uneasiness; but when he also began to run foul of the Dean it was a different story. A series of peccadilloes had led to fines and 'gatings' which had left both Scarborough and the Dean exasperated. I felt that the time had come to throw, if I could, a little oil on the troubled waters. Accordingly, I had decided as a preliminary to have ten minutes' conversation with Maurice that evening at a time when he would in

9

all probability be both alone and accessible. I walked through his outer room, which he seldom used except as a dining-room, and knocked on the door of his inner room.

'And what can the Dean do for the Senior Tutor?' said Maurice, when I had settled into one of his arm-chairs and lit a cigarette.

As I considered how best to frame my request into words, it passed through my mind how little I really knew of the character and inmost thoughts of a man who had been my colleague for fifteen years. He had had a brilliant and uniformly successful career at Oxford. In his undergraduate days he had been a distinguished athlete, but that had not prevented him from winning also his triumphs in the schools. His election to a fellowship in his own college had followed almost as a matter of course. As a don he had been equally successful; he was a thoroughly efficient teacher with power to make an unwilling pupil work; in college his advice was sound and practical; he had published two or three books which had enjoyed a considerable vogue; having some private means he was generous and he entertained on a lavish scale. The men, or a large majority of them, liked him and respected his ability. And yet, if the truth be told, I myself had never been quite able to suppress a faint feeling of irritation in his presence. He was always, so it seemed to me, a thought too successful, a shade too certain of himself. His books seemed to me too dogmatic to carry conviction: he would bludgeon down a critic or an opponent instead of meeting him with argument and persuasion. And in the man himself I seemed to detect a certain coarseness of fibre and a determination to pursue his own way which bordered upon selfishness. Though I never pried into his affairs I could not help guessing that he was a sensualist, and that, in the vacations at least, he indulged himself a thought too freely in pleasures which were hardly suited to the position he held. But I must not exaggerate. These were only misgivings which I seldom allowed myself to dwell on. I am only trying to explain why I did not, as many did, surrender entirely to his forceful personality. Instead I struggled always against a vague feeling of inferiority, which made me at the same time irritated and fretful. Friendly though he always was, he could never quite disguise a suspicion of patronage, a touch of the supercilious, in his manner towards me. He was now a man of nearly forty, still handsome and even striking in appearance, though to my eye his features seemed to have thickened and coarsened in the last few years. There was a hint now that before very long he would belong to an unattractive class – that of athletes who have run a little bit to seed.

'It's about Scarborough,' I said at length. 'I knew his father pretty well, as you know, and I promised to keep an eye on the boy. He seems to be developing into a bit of a rebel. Of course, I don't want to interfere in a matter of discipline – that's your job – but I wondered whether you couldn't treat him a bit easier. He's been gated a long time, for example, and I believe that only makes him anxious either to climb out of college at night or else to stir up riots inside. Couldn't you try to cure him by kindness for a while? He's not a bad lad really – indeed he's the sort of man that you usually like. Why not try the policy of reconciliation?'

Half-way through my rather clumsy appeal I was conscious that Maurice had not the slightest intention of acceding to my request. His expression remained perfectly good-tempered, but it reflected at the same time an entire confidence in his own judgement and a determination not to alter it in any particular. It was the expression which I particularly disliked, and which made me feel as though I was a rather tiresome schoolboy in the presence of his master.

'My dear Francis,' he said with a smile which was both friendly and yet faintly condescending, 'you really are too soft-hearted. Now look here. You say you don't want to interfere in a matter of discipline, and yet that is just what you're trying to do. No, no, don't apologize, I know you're acting from the best of motives. But you want me to let off Scarborough, partly because you know his father, partly because you like him, and partly because you don't know very much about his evil deeds. Now I do know a good deal about him, and I shall deal with him as I think best. To begin with, he's hand in glove with Garnett. Now you know as well as I do that the President took Garnett here as a favour. He's four or five years older than the rest of our men, and he lived for a couple of years on a ranch somewhere in Mexico, and God knows where else besides, after he left school. Well, there's no mad plan he won't carry out. He climbs in and out of college like a cat, he drinks more than he should, he doesn't do a stroke of work. How the poor old President was bamboozled into admitting him here I simply can't imagine. And now look at this.'

He opened a drawer of the writing-table by his side and pulled out a revolver. A faint smile of amusement passed over his face as he observed my astonishment and dismay.

'Now that revolver was brought to me this morning by Pine, and where do you think he found it?' (Pine is our Head Porter, and little that happens in St Thomas's escapes his notice. He has a wonderful flair for knowing just what is going on.) It did not seem to me that Maurice expected an answer to his question, so I waited for him to continue. 'Well,' he went on, 'Scarborough and Garnett have been complaining, rather impertinently, of the cats in the garden under their bedroom windows. Yesterday a cat was shot there; to-day Pine, who I'm bound to say is a pretty efficient man, and seldom suspects the wrong person, found this revolver in Garnett's room, together with some bullets which were in Scarborough's room next door. Where they got the thing from I don't know, but they've no shadow of excuse for being in possession of a revolver, and still less for using it. You see it's loaded still in four chambers.' He held the revolver up for my inspection. 'To-morrow morning I propose to twist the tails of those two young men – good and proper, so please, my dear Francis, don't come to me appealing for mercy. I shall, if you would like to know my private opinion, be very surprised if either of them succeeds in remaining a resident member of this college until the end of his three years! Now don't think me rude, but I really must go and dress for dinner.'

We both got up, I feeling abashed and irritated at the collapse of my negotiation. Of course Maurice was right, but I could not help feeling that in some indefinable way I had been made to appear small and ridiculous. On the way to the door I made another effort to assert my dignity.

'I hope,' I said, 'that you'll unload that revolver. To leave loaded weapons lying about is unpardonable.'

'On the contrary,' he replied, 'I shall put it exactly as it is just here,' and he laid it on a large octagonal table, which stood close to his door. 'The malefactors can then hardly fail to see it when they come into the room at nine o'clock to-morrow morning, and I shall begin by explaining to them the extreme danger involved in their conduct. But now I really must dress.'

I could hardly resist this second dismissal. In a state of considerable annoyance I walked out into the Quad and entered the Senior Common Room.

It was our custom at St Thomas's, as at most other Oxford colleges, to meet in Common Room some minutes before dinner, and to walk together from there by the small winding staircase which leads to the Hall above. We had little or no ceremony; those who were present at half-past seven would walk together to Hall; those who were late came one by one and took the vacant places at the high table there. But that night I was anxious to be in good time in order that I might make the acquaintance of a distinguished person, who was to be the guest of the college for the next week. Not infrequently foreigners of distinction are invited to Oxford to deliver learned lectures to exiguous audiences, and' during their stay are usually the guests either of friends in the University or of colleges. Of Ernst Brendel, whom I was now to meet for the first time, I knew nothing save that he was a Viennese lawyer of European reputation, who was to deliver three lectures in Oxford for the faculty of Law. Both Prendergast, our law don, and the President, who had many friends among German men of learning, had been anxious that St Thomas's should offer him hospitality. We had asked him to stay with us, and he had accepted. As Senior Tutor, I was accustomed to preside at dinner in Hall and afterwards in Common Room, for the President seldom joined us, except on Sundays. Prendergast had undertaken to meet his fellow lawyer at the station, to show him his rooms, and to bring him to dinner, but I was anxious to be in Common Room to extend a welcome to him before dinner began.

I confess that the prospect did not fill me with pleasurable anticipation. I could remember with miserable clarity previous guests who had made Common Room life burdensome for the duration of their visits – a gentleman from Sweden so taciturn as to make human intercourse almost impossible, a German so voluble as to make all thought of it abhorrent, another who discussed so persistently and exclusively his own special subject – and that an abstruse affair of physics and mathematics – that the very words *Gelehrter* and *Sachverständiger* became to me as red rags to a bull. I hoped desperately, though without much confidence, that Brendel would at least speak sufficient English to make conversation bearable, and that he would have grasped that great truth of polite society, the truth that guests have duties in entertainment no less than hosts. I opened the door and walked into the Senior Common Room.

# CHAPTER TWO

THOUGH it still wanted some ten minutes to dinner time, there were already two figures by the fire, and, as I came towards them, Prendergast stepped forward and introduced me to Brendel. In a moment all my fears and misgivings seemed to disappear. I saw before me a man rather below the middle height, but stoutly and compactly built. He appeared to be about fifty, with thick but greying hair, and glasses which twinkled in the reflexion of the lights. His dinner jacket was cut in a fashion vaguely but indefinably foreign, otherwise he had the appearance of a solid middle-aged English family lawyer. But it was not his outward appearance which immediately impressed me, nor yet his voice, though that was pleasant enough; it was rather the immediate impression which he made upon me of security and understanding. Here, I said to myself, is a man who can be trusted; a man to whom secrets will be confided, and by whom they will never be betrayed; a man who will not easily be shocked and embarrassed but who will give good counsel in times of difficulty, a man full of sympathy, who is wise and tolerant because he has looked deep into human nature. And a man with it all who is humorous and kindly as well as learned. I glanced again at his face and noted the network of wrinkles round the corners of his eyes. Yes, emphatically, a man to know as a friend and to value as a counsellor. I don't mean, of course, that all these thoughts flashed immediately through my mind – no doubt they came to me gradually – but I do mean that in all my life I have never met another man for whom I felt a more immediate liking, respect, and sympathy. I have often thought since how I could describe Brendel, and I have never succeeded to my own satisfaction. If I lay stress on his look of friendliness and good nature I should not do justice

16

to the intelligence of his face, for good nature is too often stupid. If, again, I speak of the sensation of stability and confidence with which he inspired me, I should run the risk of forgetting that he retained all the alertness of a man half his age. He belonged, I think, to that class of persons who, because they are profoundly interested in and sympathetic towards their fellow men, can never in nature grow old.

Without any of those difficult pauses and artificial conversational gambits which usually make the first five minutes in the company of a stranger almost unbearable to me we had glided into conversation, as though we had known one another for years. He spoke of life in a college at Oxford and of the undergraduates there, as though he knew instinctively where the real interests of my life lay. But already others of our society had come into the room, introductions were made, and, as half-past seven struck, we moved up to the Hall for dinner.

Only a Philistine of the first water could fail to be impressed by the beauty of the dining-hall of St Thomas's. The long tables and benches almost black with age, the lights on the tables which left the great space above dark and mysterious, the beautiful sixteenth-century roof, now only dimly seen, the rows of stately portraits along the walls; the high table where the silver showed white against the background of the bare oak table beneath it – all these made up a picture, which no amount of familiarity could ever make other than a marvel of beauty to my eyes. Brendel, seeing it for the first time, and passing a long lingering glance over it all, was visibly impressed.

'Now I think I begin to understand your Oxford traditions,' he said to me, as all the little wrinkles round his eyes showed themselves in a new pattern.

Prendergast, who was sitting on the other side, began to compliment him on his English. It was, in fact, quite exceptionally good. Now and then some slight turn of phrase or trick of intonation betrayed the foreigner, but for the most part he spoke correctly and almost without effort. 'But how should it not be good?' he answered. 'For you know I spent a year studying in London before the war, as well as a semester at the Harvard Law School, and during the war – well, I was a prisoner here for more than two years. Not all what you call a picnic, that, either,' he added with a laugh; 'but everywhere one learns as one lives.' And he began to tell Prendergast something of English prison camps.

Meanwhile I glanced round the table to see who was dining, and to compare them with the list of names which lay by my plate. I frowned a little as I noticed that we were thirteen. Naturally it happens not infrequently with our changing numbers that thirteen sit down to dine, but I am by nature superstitious, and it always gives me an irrational feeling of discomfort when I notice that particular omen of misfortune. Of those who were dining that night I have already said something of Brendel, Maurice Hargreaves, and Prendergast. On my left was Shirley, silent as usual, handsome, cold, almost grim. I have already mentioned him, but now I may say more. I never saw him without recalling that famous description of Charles X— 'He bore proudly on his shoulders the burden of his immense unpopularity.' Of all our number Shirley had perhaps the greatest reputation outside the walls of the college. He was indeed a great scholar, bold and adventurous in emendations and suggestions, but contemptuous of the views of others, and bitter and unrestrained in his criticisms of his fellows. The harshness of his character and his total lack of adaptability had prevented him time and again from receiving the recognition and advancement which were undoubtedly his due, and this fact had served only to make him more austere and more bitter. Amongst his colleagues he was at best taciturn and icily polite, at the worst cynically and even cruelly critical. And yet I could not bring myself wholly to dislike him. He was now over fifty, and I had known him for twenty-five years. I had recognized the disappointments which had marred his career, and I knew how deeply he resented teaching unwilling undergraduates, when he would fain have occupied a professorial chair. I respected his intellectual brilliance, and I had somehow contrived, though with difficulty, to avoid any open quarrel with him. He in return treated me with a kind of grudging politeness which he did not accord to most of the other tutors of St Thomas's. His books, like himself, were a compound of brilliance and bitterness. A married man, he dined seldom, and I was surprised to see him there that night.

It was with a sigh of relief that I noticed that Shepardson, our other classical tutor, was sitting at the far end of the table, and well removed from Shirley. Shepardson was keen and zealous, and a competent scholar, but he was not always very prudent, and he had recently published a book which had shown some traces of careless compilation and hasty judgements. His sanguine complexion, his face which gave an impression of size although no feature in it was at all prominent, and his high-pitched voice gave the clue to his character. He was well-meaning enough, and good-natured though easily provoked, but he was too easily gullible and often foolish. It was characteristic of Shirley that the fact that Shepardson was his colleague had not deterred him for one moment from accepting the latter's book for review. He had cut it to pieces in a savage article, in which almost every sentence was like the cut from a whip. The two men had not spoken to one another since the article appeared, and the unfortunate Shepardson vainly and almost pathetically waited for some heaven-sent opportunity for revenge. Public opinion was all on his side. We felt that Shirley had shown a lack of taste and of *esprit de corps*, but our sympathy did little to smooth down poor Shepardson, who had, after all, been publicly pilloried and held up to contempt.

I suppose that, like most of those who try to describe the characters of their acquaintances, I am easily led into exaggeration. I must guard myself, then, against over-estimating the unpopularity of Shirley. Besides myself, Maurice Hargreaves had always remained on tolerably good terms with him. The two men liked to discuss questions of classical learning and ancient history, and they had always tended to agree on matters of college policy and business. It was indeed to discuss some such matter, as I learned later, that Shirley had come in to dine that night. Furthermore, with one other of our number he was on terms which amounted almost to friendship. That other was Mottram, who now sat beside him, and their mutual liking was to me always something of an enigma. Mottram had been a scholar at one of the smaller colleges, had studied medicine and had been appointed to a research fellowship at St Thomas's after a series of consistently brilliant examinations in the schools. We had been told when we elected him that he was destined for scientific eminence, perhaps for European fame. Socially, however, Mottram was hardly a success. He was shy and silent, sometimes almost *farouche*. In manner he seemed almost always to be on the defensive, and he had little or none of the easy companionability of most of the men of his generation. A doctor would have noticed at once that he was a myope – and he suffered, perhaps for that reason, from an inferiority complex, which tended to increase rather than to diminish as he grew older. Most of his time was spent in his laboratory, he cared little for sport or literature or society, and after a time he sank as it were into the background of our Common Room life. Like the furniture, we accepted his presence without comment; we should possibly have noticed his absence had he been away for a term, his presence we hardly remarked at all. And yet I sometimes felt that in him hidden fires were smouldering. Very, very occasionally some stray remark would indicate that his mind was occupied with strong ideas and vital issues. I guessed, though dimly, that this silent and retiring man had also depths of thought and feeling which he concealed from the world in which he lived. Curiously enough something like friendship had sprung up between him and Shirley, widely different though their interests were. Perhaps the natural aloofness of each was a bond between them, perhaps each recognized and admired instinctively the intellectual quality of the other. In any case, Mottram spoke more freely and more often to Shirley than to any of the rest of us, and Shirley treated him in return with respect and even almost with amiability. I had even heard him, in Mottram's absence, defend the latter from criticism with a kind of warmth and feeling.

Of the others who were dining that night there is less to say. The Bursar, Major Trower, was there, most military in manner and possessing a soldierly brusqueness of speech, which entirely belied his natural kindliness of heart. All the younger men were genuinely fond of him, and delighted in the harmless pastime of pulling his leg. For his part the 'brutal and licentious soldier', as they liked to call him, was entirely happy among them, and spent his whole time and energy in increasing the material comforts and social harmony of the college. As befitted one of his profession his bark was prodigious, but his bite was antiseptic. Farther along was a little group of three, Dixon, a physicist, Whitaker, our mathematical tutor, and a guest of his from Balliol, whose name I had not heard. All three were deep in some scientific discussion, quite meaningless to me. Two others completed the party. John Doyne, the Junior Dean, cheerful, ruddy-complexioned and perpetually laughing, was everybody's friend, and the enemy of none. No don and no undergraduate was able to resist his infectious high spirits. Lastly there was little Mitton, our chaplain, rather pink and white in appearance, and prone to blushing, a failing which filled him with embarrassment and everyone else with amusement. He was not a bad fellow, though apt to be spiky and cantankerous where ecclesiastical questions were involved. He had not quite enough humour to defend himself adequately against the playful assaults of some of his colleagues. Prendergast, I regret to say, took an unholy pleasure in ragging him and exciting his blushes. The undergraduates, with their flair for choosing nicknames both appropriate and inappropriate, called him 'the frozen mitt', a name which, for some obscure reason, filled the little man with an unreasonable annoyance. Prendergast, with desire to tease, would sometimes announce his intention of 'thawing the frozen mitt', a remark which never failed to bring the desired blush to the chaplain's cheeks.

Taken together, a set of men such as might have been seen at any high table at Oxford that night. But I have been compelled to describe them in some detail, for each one of them, little though he knew it, was by the accident of his presence there that evening, destined to be involved more or less intimately in a grim drama of tragedy and crime.

I looked up from the list of diners, and heard the Bursar asking the Dean whether he expected much noise and excitement in college that night. The question was a not unnatural one. I have often maintained, and am still prepared to do so, that it would be difficult to find a better behaved and more reasonable set of young men than the undergraduates at Oxford as a whole, and St Thomas's in particular. Contrary to the ideas which are sometimes promulgated by the cheaper newspapers, and by authors of these Oxford novels whose foible would appear to be the crime of Almamatricide, scenes of riot and disorder are almost unknown; so too is habitual drunkenness. But there are times when authority turns a blind eye to a certain amount of high-spirited rejoicing, and to-night was one of these occasions. For it was the Wednesday night after the last day of the Torpids. After six days of racing which had followed a long and severe period of training it would not be in human nature to refrain from some sort of celebration. Besides, both our boats had done well; both of them had gone up several places – not enough, it is true, to warrant the official recognition of a Bump Supper, but enough to induce a feeling of legitimate exultation. No doubt there would be a considerable turmoil in the Quad, a certain number of fireworks would fly into the air, and a certain proportion of those who had just come out of training would become noisily, if only mildly, intoxicated. Such scenes one could afford to treat with tolerance.

Maurice answered the Bursar's question carelessly. 'Oh, I don't think so,' he said. 'There might be a bit of noise and even a few broken windows. Perhaps some of them will try to start a bonfire, but if they do J. D. will have to go out and stop it.'

Doyne grinned. He really rather enjoyed quelling scenes of disorder, for his good temper made his interference effective, and he liked the exercise of authority.

The mention of possible undergraduate excesses recalled Scarborough and Garnett to Maurice Hargreaves' mind, and he began to relate their misdoings at some length to his neighbours. He liked to tell a story, and their misdeeds lost nothing in the telling. His voice was powerful and peculiarly resonant, and I noticed that the whole table was listening to him. The episode of the revolver made a real sensation, and even Shirley seemed to think that its use was something of an outrage. Personally I was growing more and more annoyed. It seemed to me improper as well as unfair to give these young men a bad name and so hang them, as it were, out of hand. So I suppose there was irritation in my voice when I spoke to Maurice, as he completed his tale.

23

'I do wish that you wouldn't leave that loaded revolver lying on the table just inside your room,' I said. 'It's childish to say that you mean to use it as the text for a lecture on the danger of lethal weapons to-morrow morning, and it's positively dangerous to leave it loaded where it is.'

'My dear Francis,' he answered, 'you really are, if I may say so with all due respect, tending to become the least bit of an old woman. For consider . . .' He ticked off the points as he made them on his fingers. 'One, it is only in books that loaded firearms go off. In my limited experience it requires some human agency to pull the trigger. Two. There are no children, women, or imbeciles within the walls of this college. Three. What grown man would point a revolver at himself or at any other living creature before he pulled the trigger to discover whether it was loaded? And four. I have sported the oak of my rooms, and the key lies safely in my pocket. Is the peril which you suggest really so very imminent?'

His easy bantering tone had its usual effect on me. I felt both impotent to reply and irritated at my own insignificance.

'Well,' I said, 'it can't be right to leave loaded weapons lying about. If someone's shot don't say that I didn't warn you. I was brought up in the belief that all firearms are loaded and that all horses kick, and that both are dangerous. A very good lesson to teach a boy, too!' I turned to Brendel, anxious to change the conversation.

'Do you know that before I came in I was quite frightened about you,' I said. 'I expected to be either overwhelmed with learning, or else compelled to carry on an interchange of polite inanities in a language which I know very imperfectly.'

All the little wrinkles showed round his eyes. 'And you find the foreign professor not all too alarming?' he answered with a smile.

24

'On the contrary; and conversation a pleasure instead of a burden.'

He made me a quaint little half bow. 'Thank you. I also. But you know I was perhaps a little nervous too – one poor lawyer from Vienna and a dozen great English professors!'

'Yes,' I said, 'I can understand that. I remember a rather famous admiral dining here one night. He was the best company you can imagine, and kept us all in roars of laughter the whole evening. I never saw anyone who captured a roomful of people so quickly or held them all so easily. What the moderns call getting it across. As he was going away I thanked him for the pleasure his yarns had given us. "Well," he said, "you know when I arrived I was in the devil of a fright at spending the evening among a crew of highbrows, but as I came into your Common Room I heard a white-haired old professor complaining bitterly to a sympathetic circle of the price of bottled beer, and I felt at home right away. Human nature doesn't vary much when you get down to fundamental issues like the price of beer."'

Brendel chuckled. 'That's it,' he said. 'We've generally got plenty in common with everyone we meet if only we'll let ourselves talk about it. Now I feel a kind of fascination when you begin to talk of loaded revolvers, for, you see, the study of crime and its detection is my passion. Yes, that kind of thing is really my one great hobby. What did your Lord Birkenhead write? "I have surrendered myself often and willingly to the deception of the detective tale." Something like that, wasn't it? Well, I suppose that I've read almost every good detective tale that has ever been written, and a good many thousand bad ones as well, and all that only as a kind of appetizer to the study of the true tale of crime. There's no great murder trial of the last twenty years that I've not followed from start to finish – and in one or two of them – well, I had some small part to play myself.'

'By Jove, that's interesting,' said Doyne, who was listening from the other side of the table. 'You must tell us more about this, Professor. We thought that you were just an ordinary man of prodigious learning, and now we find that we are entertaining an angel unawares. A new Sherlock Holmes from Vienna, with all the modern improvements. You'll find that everyone in this Common Room has a theory of his own about the art of detection, especially Mitton, who thinks that Providence always leads the culprit to repentance and confession about three days after the crime.'

Mitton became so alarmingly pink at this garbled account of his views that I thought it best to break off the discussion. Dinner was over, so I got up and said grace. Then we trooped together down to Common Room.

# CHAPTER THREE

To a middle-aged don, as I might describe myself, or to an old don, as I might almost be described, there is no place more pleasant than Common Room, no hour more wholly pleasurable than that spent in it immediately after dinner. For here the Fellows of St Thomas's, having dined, settled down to enjoy the comfort of port and dessert, of coffee and cigars. I had come, as I grew older, to look forward all day to that hour in the evening which I most enjoyed. The good wine, the flow of conversation, the ritual of the table at once dignified and almost stately and yet homely as well, exercised a soothing effect on my nerves and filled me with a sense of physical and mental well-being. Providence gave me, I think, an imperfect appreciation of the beauties of nature; I can't enthuse over the grandeur of hills or seas, nor even over the more placid loveliness of the countryside. But as some sort of compensation I have a real aesthetic love of the lighted interior, the scene of social intercourse and good fellowship at their best. For me a Dutch interior by Maes or Terborch, or an eighteenth-century conversation piece is worth more than any landscape or seascape that was ever painted. Nor was it only the externals of the Common Room which I loved; it seemed rather that life there suited itself to my every mood. If I felt festive and sociable there were always others ready to meet me halfway. If on the other hand a black shadow of pessimism was on me, the room seemed to attune itself to me. I thought of it then as the home of a multitude of my predecessors – who had drunk their wine and lived their short lives there since the foundation of the college. A sorrowful thought, made more poignant by that deep misgiving from which few can escape.

*Ah, but the Apparition – the dumb sign –*
*The beckoning finger bidding me forgo*
*The fellowship, the converse and the wine,*
*The songs, the festal glow!*
*And ah, to know not, while with friends I sit*
*And while the purple joy is pass'd about,*
*Whether 'tis ampler day divinelier lit,*
*Or homeless night without.*

How well that great but misjudged modern poet voices my
blacker mood! But that mood was rare. For the most part
I was supremely contented and happy in that place. The
Common Room of St Thomas's was indeed my spiritual
home. In earlier days I had been accustomed to work after
dinner, but now I tended more and more to sit talking
and smoking until it was time for a book and bed.

I moved to my seat at the end of the table, where the
decanters and the snuff lay before me, and invited Brendel
to sit at my right hand. On the other side of me I put
Whitaker's guest. The rest of the party seated themselves
as they pleased. I observed with a good deal of satisfaction
that the younger members moved quickly to sit near the
Viennese; it was obvious that they had capitulated to his
charm of manner as easily as had I.

Hardly had we settled down, and the wine begun its
first leisurely journey round the table, when Doyne reminded Brendel of his remark in Hall.

'You must tell us more about your views on detection,
Professor. Here we all belong to different schools of thought.
Apart from Mitton, who has a school of his own, simple
faith and all will come well, you know' (the chaplain made
an inarticulate murmur of protest which passed unheeded),
'we're really divided into three groups. Let me see. There
are Dixon and Whitaker, who belong to the pseudo-
scientific school. They've discarded cigarette ends and heel-
marks as belonging to an earlier age, but they still believe

28

that by picking up hairs and putting them under micro-
scopes they can prove that the murder has been committed
by a man of about fifty-five, going bald at the temples.
Prendergast and I, on the other hand, believe in sitting in
arm-chairs and smoking pipes, until we have discussed all
the possible murderers and their motives. We then get up
and point with unerring finger at the guilty man. Lastly,
there's the Bursar, who believes in official methods and
the trained detective. He would have everyone who was
within half a mile of the murder lined up and presented
with a questionnaire of the most searching description.
The man who can't answer the questions to the Major's
satisfaction is the murderer. What could be simpler? Now,
Professor, which school gets your vote? Are you for clues,
or are you for logical deduction, or are you for military
methods and death at dawn?'

We all laughed, Brendel with us. I could see that he
liked the young and their talk. Yet his answer, when it
came, was carefully phrased and his tone was oddly serious.

'You must forgive me,' he said, 'if I take it all a little
more seriously than that. I said that I read detective tales,
and so I do, but that's only as a kind of relaxation. What
fascinates me, yes at times obsesses me, is the real crime –
the murder that has actually been committed. Listen.' (I
had already noticed that Brendel had a habit of saying
'listen' in a curiously compelling tone of voice before any
sentence which he regarded as especially important.) 'I
must beg leave to tell you gentlemen how I came to be
immersed in that special study. I was a young lawyer in
Vienna, and a client of mine was murdered, suddenly,
horribly, inexplicably. I was drawn into the investigations
which followed; I could not escape from them. And
gradually there was unfolded before my eyes a drama of
feeling and passion, of hidden desires and secret motives,
of a sort that I had never dreamed of. It so happened that

I saw more clearly than the rest; I was able to suggest a line of investigation that led eventually to the arrest of the murderer. Through that I won a sort of . . . .' He hesitated for a moment for a word. '*Renommée?*'

'Reputation,' said someone.

'Yes, reputation. How ridiculous it is that one suddenly fails to find the simplest word when one is speaking a language not one's own. I acquired a sort of reputation. The police consulted me not once but many times; sometimes I could help them, often I could not. And so I learned the grammar and the syntax of murder.'

He paused for a minute, and seemed to be diving into his memories.

'Have you ever really considered,' he went on, 'the drama behind a murder, the play of human passions, the desperation, the daring? And think of the stake at issue! Your scientist can do most things, but he can't create life, and it is life that you are, by one quick act, taking away. And to take it you risk everything; not just your future or your goods or even your happiness, but everything you have – everything – your own life! And remember, once the stake is thrown on the board it cannot be removed. What gamble is there comparable to that, a gamble in human life?' He held up his forefinger almost menacingly as he spoke, and his voice had grown harsh with suppressed feeling.

In a moment he went on in a quieter voice, 'Of course, I am speaking of the real murders, the murders that are planned and contrived and executed with intention. I don't mean those wretched crimes of brute violence, when some poor fellow is knocked on the head for the sake of a few pounds. They're just sordid and wretched. No, nor your American crimes either.' He smiled and glanced round the room. I think that he wanted to be sure that there was no American among us, whose susceptibilities he might offend.

'I love America and the Americans; they're the kindest and most hospitable . . .' He checked himself abruptly and his smile became a little chuckling laugh.

'So I've nearly, oh, so nearly – but what's your odd expression for making a mistake?'

'Dropped a brick,' said Doyne, laughing with him.

'That's it. Dropped a brick.' He repeated it slowly as though memorizing it for future use. 'My poor little brick, you must forgive it. Well, I should have said that nowhere except at Oxford is there hospitality to compare with that of the Americans. But when it comes to crime, why then I find them just a little vulgar. "Bump off, shoot up," what expressions!' He shrugged his shoulders with an ineffable suggestion of distaste. 'Of course some of you know Theodore Dreiser's *American Tragedy*; that's a great book. I learned much from that. But somehow I still believe that the newer countries have not risen to great murders yet; they seem to lack the dignity, the aristocratic touch.'

'The dignity of murder,' said Prendergast, 'not a bad title that, for a book.'

'When you've cut out all the casual crimes, all these modern senseless slaughters,' Brendel went on, 'you're left with murders that are worth study – the great murders; and it's then that detection becomes a great art, too. And the motives. Sometimes it's love of gain. At first the desire for wealth and all that it brings with it, and then the birth of temptation – the realization, perhaps, that one frail life stands between a man and all his material desires – and after that slowly, slowly, the growth of the idea, and finally the great gamble, the murder itself. Or sometimes it's just hatred, sheer personal hatred, which grows and grows until it becomes an overmastering passion. And sometimes that hatred has begun from something in itself so trivial that only a psycho-analyst could trace it. Think of a man married to a woman whom he does not love; think of some

31

small action at first only an irritation, and then, repeated day by day, a burden, a cancer, a disease worse than death! And then the thought of freedom, at first only a hope, then a plan, then an overmastering impulse. Yes, some murders have grown from what we lightly call incompatibility. Or again there's sexual jealousy, jealousy that distorts the vision and blinds the judgement till it leads the straight way to disaster and to death. But all murders, using the word as I do, have this in common. They're the result of long preparation, or desperate planning, of the struggle of some tortured soul for freedom at any cost. And that's where the detective comes in; he's like a historian, tracing the hidden threads, diving into the forgotten past, exposing the plans and the motives of men, or like a surgeon, cutting down deep into a malignant growth, till at last he reaches its hidden source and origin. Do you see what I mean?'

'I think I appreciate the point about the little sources of friction, and all that at the beginning,' said Maurice Hargreaves with a laugh. 'When I first came to St Thomas's I remember being told a story about old Fothergill, who was still about the place though he must have been pretty well eighty. Winn and Shirley will have heard the story before, but that doesn't matter. Well, Fothergill, about twenty years before, had had a scout, and that scout disappeared. One day he was there doing his job, and the next he just wasn't. He disappeared altogether and no one ever saw him again. There was no explanation, and there never has been, but gradually a legend grew up, and finally everyone accepted it as part of the college history. What had happened, so the legend went, was this. When Fothergill was first appointed to his fellowship his scout brought him two fried eggs for breakfast. Fothergill couldn't stand fried eggs at any price, but he was terribly shy and frightened of his scout, and so he ate both the eggs and said nothing. The scout thought that he had found out, first guess, what Fothergill really liked for breakfast. He ordered fried eggs the next morning, and Fothergill ate them again. So then the scout made it a standing order. Every day Fothergill tried to make up his mind to speak, and every day it became more difficult. How could he say after a month of fried eggs that he had only eaten them because he was afraid of saying that he hated them? Gradually he got a dreadful inferiority complex; he loathed the eggs; he couldn't tell the scout so. And that went on for twenty years. At last he couldn't bear it any longer and one night when his scout came in with his whisky after dinner he quietly murdered him, and buried him that night in the college meadow. Next morning, when his scout didn't turn up, the man on the next stair came instead to call Fothergill, and to ask if there were any orders. "A hot bath and sausages for breakfast," said Fothergill, and then went to sleep again for another half-hour.'

Maurice's story had relieved the tension, and I felt glad that he had told it, for Brendel had spoken with so much feeling that I feared the discussion was tending to become too serious to be altogether pleasant. Prendergast, however, who had hung on the Professor's words ever since he had come into Common Room, had no intention of allowing the main topic to drop.

'Do you think,' he said, 'that a real murderer, the sort of murderer that you have described, often escapes?'

'Hardly ever,' said Brendel. 'How often is the murderer equal to his task? He is often ignorant of the methods or the implements which he must use, he often makes some elementary mistake, he is often destroyed by some unforeseen accident, some chance encounter or some unlucky remark. And there's another point, too. Have you ever considered how well, how intimately, you must know a man to murder him?'

'No, never,' said little Mitton involuntarily, though the question had not been directed specially to him.

'Think about that, then. They say that a man ought to know a woman well when he marries her, but how much better must the true murderer know his victim? He studies his every action and his every thought. He watches him from day to day, plotting and observing. His whole mind is filled and obsessed by the thought of his victim; he knows him as well as and better than he knows himself. And because men have few intimates, and because the society in which any man lives is small, it follows that the possible murderers of any one man are very, very few. A detective should never forget the importance of propinquity when he's searching for the murderer. It's the first essential, the necessary condition of guilt. Strangers don't commit murders, though they may do acts of violence. Yet with all these difficulties the thing you suggest can be done. Listen. We are all intelligent men here – we may say that without conceit – if one of us planned a murder he could carry it out, and he could, if he would only be patient enough, carry it out without being discovered. For the cold passionless man of science can surely destroy traces and leave no clues. Only his nerve must be steel, and his patience the patience of Job.'

'Do you think that the successful murderer plans his whole crime from beginning to end before he acts at all?' said Dixon.

'Sometimes, but not always. In the poison cases he often does. But there is another type as well, the type that makes up his mind, and then waits and waits and waits until fate throws into his hands the perfect opportunity to strike. He is the most dangerous of them all – the cold-blooded murderer, who has the patience to wait as well as the will to kill.'

As he finished his sentence the door opened and Callender, the Common Room butler, entered the room with coffee. I had not rung, but he had orders to bring in coffee at twenty minutes to nine if it had not been ordered before. I could not help feeling glad of the interruption, for whatever the others might think I was myself definitely uncomfortable at the turn which the conversation had taken. I should much have preferred to discuss the rival merits of the ports of the great vintage years than the motives of even the most 'dignified' murderers.

*

Shepardson drank his coffee quickly and got up from the table. 'I'm sorry,' he said, 'I must go. I've got a couple of pupils at a quarter to nine.'

'Rather severe, isn't it,' said Doyne, 'to take them on the last night of toggers?'

'Oh, no. It's only Howe and Martin. Neither of them are rowing men, and to-night's as good as any other evening for them, or as bad, for that matter, for I can't get much work out of either of them.'

'I must go, too. I want to go up to my Lab.,' said Mottram.

He got up and followed Shepardson from the room. It was Mottram's habit to work in the laboratory, which was in South Parks Road, four or five evenings in the week. Sometimes he went early, sometimes late, often he stayed for the greater part of the night. He kept a small Morris two-seater, which he used to leave just outside college before dinner, and which often remained out of doors all night.

I watched him go with a feeling both of sympathy and pity. It is true that I did not know him well, and that I was totally ignorant of the nature of his work. Besides, his silence and his shyness made contact with him difficult, and intimacy impossible. But I did know that a week or two before a shattering blow had fallen on him, and I wished from the bottom of my heart that I knew how to assist and befriend him. For four years Mottram had been engaged on a piece of difficult and most important research; if it was successful he would have in his hands the cure for one of the most dangerous of diseases. He had worked day by day with unfaltering application, and had refused to be deterred by many set-backs and many disappointments. He had refrained, too, from those publications of partial results by which many scientists are wont to advertise their industry and acquire a reputation for learning. After about three years of endeavour Mottram seemed to be within sight of success; Dixon, who was in touch with the medical faculty, had kept me posted as to the progress of the research, and had told me with growing excitement that after a few more months, to satisfy himself of the accuracy of his results, Mottram would be in a position to give his discovery to the world. And then, quite suddenly, the blow fell. A German in Freiburg, who had apparently been following much the same line of investigation, published in a leading journal, and with great flourish of trumpets, a paper describing his researches and their results. There was, so Dixon sorrowfully informed me, only one conclusion. Mottram's work was now superfluous. Some few additions he might indeed contribute; but the main credit, the honour for which he had striven, had gone elsewhere. He took the blow well, indeed many of his acquaintances knew nothing of it. But for the last weeks he had become even more silent, more retiring, more aloof than before, and I felt miserably certain that he felt what had occurred as a catastrophe. I had made one attempt at commiseration, and had been firmly, almost rudely, rebuffed. He said rather grimly that such things happened, and that it really mattered little since the benefit to humanity was the same whether it came from Freiburg or Oxford, and he wanted no sympathy. To me the whole thing seemed cruel and unfair. Some of the members of our Common Room, notably Maurice Hargreaves, had been inclined to scoff a little at our brilliant medical researcher, who never produced any results. I felt that all their criticisms, which ought to have been silenced by a great achievement, would now gain in volume and in power to hurt.

We had moved from the table to the fire when coffee was finished, and were smoking contentedly whilst behind us Callender and his boy were busy clearing away the fruit and glasses and all the débris of dessert. Brendel had wished, I saw, to lead the conversation into other channels, but Hargreaves, Prendergast, and Doyne were obviously keenly interested in his criminal investigations and had begged him to tell them something of some of the cases which had occupied his attention in Vienna. He gave way good-temperedly enough, and I, too, became enthralled as he unfolded to us the history of a poisoning mystery, of which I remembered to have read a brief and garbled account in my paper some few weeks before. More and more I had the impression that in Brendel were combined many of the qualities that I most admired. He seemed to unite an instinctive sympathy with his fellow-men with an astonishing power of piercing to the essentials of every problem. I found myself wondering what Shirley's intellect might not have accomplished if he could have added to it something of this visitor's broad humanity and patience.

Nine o'clock struck, and Shirley himself, who had been listening keenly but saying little, rose to his feet.

'Hargreaves,' he said, 'I came in to dine really to see all the new library plans and discuss them with you. Are you ready for them now? I mustn't be too late in getting home.'

We were planning to enlarge our library, and a great deal of ink had been spilt in the discussion of new plans. Hargreaves and Shirley had taken a leading part, and had together championed a more extensive alteration than the rest of us desired. They had at length converted a majority of us in principle to their way of thinking, and now the new plans together with a voluminous report from the architects and a mass of suggestions and annotations had arrived for consideration. Hargreaves was an enthusiast for what he called 'the big plan,' and I expected him to get up at once, but he was never a person to consider the comfort of others before his own, and now he was thoroughly enjoying Brendel's reminiscences. Instead of getting up, therefore, he pulled a key from his pocket and gave it to Shirley.

'Here's the key of my oak,' he said, 'all the stuff about the library is on my writing-table. I wish you'd look through it all and compare the different suggestions. I'd like to know if you come independently to the same conclusions as I did. I'll be with you in less than half an hour.'

Shirley nodded, and took the key.

'Don't play with the loaded revolver on my table,' Hargreaves shouted after him – for my benefit I felt, rather than for Shirley's.

But I wasted no time in ruminating over Maurice's lack of taste. If he liked to make fun of what he called my old-womanliness he could. I was content to sit back in my arm-chair and give myself up the pleasure of listening to Brendel. Only those, I think, who live the sheltered academic life can enjoy to the full the recital of the events of the world outside.

But even in the academic world, alarms and excursions must sometimes occur. We had been talking for what seemed to me only a short time when a knock came at the door, and the Head Porter entered.

'If you please, Sir,' he said, 'there's a lot of noise and breaking going on in the Quad, and some of the gentlemen are trying to light a bonfire. Could you come out, Sir?'

'Bother,' said Maurice. 'You'd better go, J.D., and drive them home to their beds. I want to hear the end of this.'

Doyne got up obediently and put on his cap and gown. 'Right,' he said, 'I'll be back later on, Professor, to hear the end of that story.' Whitaker and his guest, together with Dixon, left at the same time. They had been plunged for the last half-hour in a scientific discussion and proposed to adjourn to Whitaker's rooms to consult the work of some scientific pundit to settle their argument. I glanced at the clock and was amazed to see that it was already a quarter to ten.

Our Common Room did not open directly on the Quadrangle; there was a long passage with a door at either end, and our windows looked out upon a small garden. But in spite of the distance I had been subconsciously aware for some time of shouts of elation and revelry in the distance. I had heard the distant explosion of fireworks, and noises which sounded suspiciously like pistol-shots. No doubt someone was discharging one of those pistols which excited coaches fire off on the tow-path to encourage their crews. With Doyne's exit all the noise ceased. Discipline at St Thomas's, if not especially rigid, was undoubtedly efficient, and I could without difficulty visualize the scene outside. On Doyne's appearance the undergraduates would lose very little time in retreating to the back Quad or to their rooms. Doyne would wait a few minutes, chatting with the porter, then he would stroll into the back Quad to see that no damage was being done, and then, if all was in order, he would return to us in Common Room. Brendel, I noticed with amusement, was taking it all in. Very little indeed, as I now knew, escaped his notice.

'Your Mr Doyne knows how to control young men,' he said approvingly to Hargreaves, 'although he looks so young. Englishmen have always had that secret.'

'It's tradition, I think,' said Maurice. 'In some colleges I think the Deans don't find it quite so easy.'

As ten o'clock struck Prendergast heaved himself unwillingly out of his arm-chair.

'You must forgive me,' he said, 'I must go up to my rooms. I promised to meet a man there at ten, to give him some books.' Trower and Mitton went out together at the same time.

Brendel would have gone too, but I stopped him. 'Another cigar,' I said, 'before we break up. It's early yet, and the fire's just burning properly. The old open fire has its merits, and you must learn to appreciate them whilst you're with us.'

He sat down again, not unwillingly, between Maurice and myself, and lit a fresh cigar with care and appreciation.

It was, I suppose, about ten minutes later that Maurice suddenly uttered an ejaculation of dismay.

'Good Heavens,' he said, 'I promised Shirley not to keep him waiting for more than half an hour, and it's an hour or more since he went. I wonder if he's still there.'

He jumped up and left us. Brendel and I were alone in the Common Room. As we sat there by the fire, I felt an extraordinary feeling of well-being and contentment. Early in the evening I had been irritated by Maurice, and unpleasantly excited by the discussion on murder and murderers, but now I felt that the world was an agreeable place indeed. My cigar was drawing to perfection; I had mixed myself a whisky and soda; the fire burned brightly and warmly; opposite to me the light twinkled on Brendel's glasses. Never had I felt more wholly at peace with all mankind. And so we sat for, I suppose, about ten minutes. Then suddenly the door was flung open, and Maurice Hargreaves lurched into the room.

'My God,' he cried. 'Come up quickly. Someone's shot Shirley – in my rooms.'

As I got to my feet my eyes turned towards Brendel. He had taken off his glasses, and was wiping them very carefully with a silk pocket-handkerchief.

# CHAPTER FOUR

HARGREAVES' rooms were on the first floor of a staircase only some forty or fifty yards from the door of the Common Room, yet I have no clear recollection of how the three of us found our way from one place to the other. I think that I must have run faster than I have run for twenty years, and I have a vague idea that Brendel followed more slowly behind me, but I cannot be sure. I am only certain of the one fact – that at one moment I had been sitting smoking and sipping my whisky and soda in complete contentment, at peace with all the world, and at the next I stood helpless and utterly horrified in the Dean's inner room.

Every detail of that set of rooms was familiar to me. Traditionally they were always occupied by the Dean of the college and I had myself lived in them for two short years, when, as a young man, I had been induced against my better judgement to accept the office of Dean. Two short years only, for the enforcement of discipline had irked and worried me, and I had gladly resigned the charge into stronger hands than my own. The set consisted in all of four rooms together with a bathroom and lobby; in front, looking out upon the main quadrangle, were two sitting-rooms. The outer one was inconvenient, in that the oak, or outer door of the set, opened directly into it, and because it was a passage room through to the inner room. Maurice Hargreaves, following the example of his predecessors, used to use the outer room as a dining-room, and the inner as a place in which to live and work. Behind these two rooms, and facing on to a small courtyard, were the bedrooms – Maurice's which was behind his inner room, and a guest-room which came next to it, and which was rather smaller. There was also a bathroom, a long passagelike lobby, and a servant's pantry, behind the outer room. Like many sets of rooms in Oxford, the arrangement was in many ways extremely inconvenient. When I had lived there myself I had been constantly annoyed by the number of doors, and by the fact that almost all the rooms led into one another. In addition the lobby was almost pitch-dark, for, except when the electric light was turned on, it was lighted only by means of a skylight at its east end which opened on to the stairs. It was also, as I had found, in the highest degree inconvenient that the only entry to the rest of the rooms, including of course the bedrooms, was through the dining-room, which was consequently itself of very little practical use. A rough sketch will make my meaning plain. In it the doors are clearly shown.

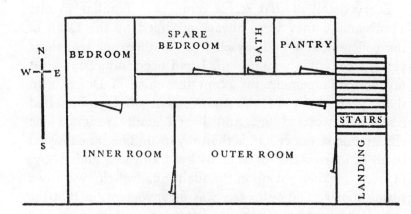

MAIN QUADRANGLE

Yet in spite of its drawbacks I could not deny that the set of rooms as a whole was redeemed from mediocrity by what I have called the inner room, which, as Maurice Hargreaves had arranged it, I must now describe. Entering by the door from the outer room a visitor would at once notice that the fire-place was situated diagonally opposite to him, and in the corner of the room. This rather curious architectural feature dictated the arrangement of the furniture, for round it were grouped four large leather armchairs, whilst the main part of the floor-space was clear of furniture. The windows, which opened into the main quadrangle, faced almost due south, so that on fine days the room was flooded with sunlight; there were two large and very lofty windows, and between them a beautiful tallboy of which Hargreaves was inordinately proud. Against the west wall, in the corner nearest the quadrangle, stood a handsome writing-table, littered with papers and with a reading-lamp on one corner; the whole of the east wall and a great part of the north wall of the room were covered by bookshelves which ran up almost to the ceiling. I have left to the last what was, to me, the most impressive feature of the room – an octagonal table of beautiful workmanship, which stood almost midway between the door from the outer room and the door into the bedroom. It had been bequeathed to these rooms in perpetuity by a former dean, and stood always in the same place, an object of admiration and pride to one dean after another. Once more I must insert a plan so that the details of the arrangement of the inner room may be absolutely clear. (See p. 44.)

Every detail of that room was, as I have already said, familiar to me, and a single glance showed it to me as I had always known it – with one ghastly exception – for in the armchair nearest to the writing table sprawled the body of Shirley.

He sat low in the chair, his head just showing above the back, and half turned to the right as though he had been in the act of turning round when he had been shot. His head had sagged forward on to his chest, and his general appearance was that of a man who had sunk in a dishevelled condition into an arm-chair. The studs in the front of his soft dress shirt were undone, and to me he gave the impression of a man partly intoxicated who had flung himself down to rest. A second glance made it obvious that he was not drunk

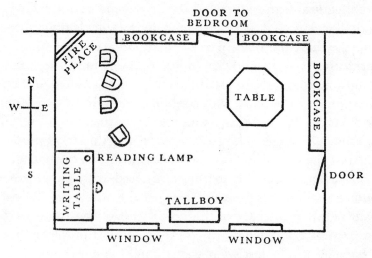

MAIN QUADRANGLE

but dead. On the right side of his head I could just see a tiny hole, not larger than a threepenny bit; on the left side was a much larger hole, a little ragged. There was hardly any blood. Instinctively my eyes turned to the octagonal table; in the middle of it, like some grim emblem of destruction, lay the revolver.

From the moment that we reached the room, Brendel seemed to take command of the situation. He took one slow comprehensive look at the room as though he would photograph every detail of it upon his mind. Then he spoke with a new note of decision and command in his voice.

'Don't touch the body, and whatever you do, don't touch the revolver. Mr Hargreaves, tell me quickly. Is there any back door, any entrance into these rooms except by the way we have come?'

'No, none whatever.'

'Then you, Mr Winn, stand in that outer room, please, by the door, whilst we search the other rooms.'

Two minutes sufficed to prove that no one was hidden in the bedrooms or the lobby.

44

'Now,' said Brendel, as we re-entered the inner room, 'tell me, as quickly as you can, please, exactly what you did since you left us?'

For the first time I realized that Maurice had left us a good ten minutes ago. Why ever had he been so long? He seemed to pull himself together, and spoke now with comparative calmness.

'I walked into the Quad,' he said, 'and I saw from below that the lights in my room were burning, so I knew that Shirley was still there, waiting for me. I met Pine – Pine is the Head Porter, you know – and had a word with him. I asked him about the noise earlier on in the Quad. And then, well, I thought that Shirley had waited a long time anyhow, and a few more minutes wouldn't matter – and it was a beautiful night – so I strolled a couple of times round the Quad before I went up. I wanted ... I wanted to think what I was going to say to Shirley, I suppose. Then I went up, and oh my God! – I saw him in the chair, like that —'

He turned his head away from the chair.

'Thank you,' said Brendel. 'You touched nothing – not the body, nor the revolver?'

Hargreaves shook his head. 'I couldn't have,' he said with a kind of shudder.

Brendel nodded. 'You have a telephone? Call the police at once, and a doctor.'

Under the influence of the Professor's calm efficiency, Maurice was rapidly recovering his poise.

'It would be better,' he said, 'to telephone from the Lodge. My line is only an extension, and anyone in the Lodge can hear what is said here.'

'I'll go,' I said hastily. I wanted to get out of that room, and I wanted insistently to do something practical.

'All right. Send Pine up here too,' Maurice replied.

I hurried across to the Lodge. As I did so I heard a few shouts and a belated firework exploding in the back Quad, a grisly reminder of revels which suddenly seemed to me queerly indecent and misplaced. It is odd how, in moments of crisis, the mind works. I ought, I suppose, to have been filled with thoughts of the tragedy of this life so suddenly and horribly ended, or of the briefness and uncertainty of all human affairs. But I was not. Miserably I was conscious that I could think only of myself. Should I do the right thing? Should I behave in these strange circumstances as befitted a man of character and intelligence, or should I appear, when the inquiries were made, to have lost my head like any other second-rate man? A wretched confession, yet, if this is to be a true story, I cannot conceal it. As I entered the Lodge my doubts and uncertainties took a practical form. Ought I to telephone first to the doctor or to the police? Which was the more important? Why could not I think out clearly even a matter so simple as that? I decided for the police; after all Shirley was indubitably dead, and no doctor could help him now, but the sooner the police were on the scene the better. I got through to the station, and hurriedly and incoherently I told some unknown police officer what had occurred, and implored him to hurry. I shouted to Pine, who was outside, to wait by the gate till the police arrived, and then to take them to the Dean's room. In answer to his unspoken question I said, 'Murder, I think,' in a voice which sounded oddly unlike my own. Then I opened the telephone directory to look up the number of one of the Oxford doctors.

At once I felt that I had been wrong. Of course it should have been the doctor first. Could not a skilful doctor tell, if he arrived in time, how long a man had been dead? Was it not of paramount importance that the time of the murder should be settled beyond possibility of mistake so that the criminal might be discovered? How many times had I not read that in works of fiction? Desperately I tried to think which of the doctors lived nearest to St Thomas's. All of them of whom I could think lived in Holywell or St Giles's or even farther away. Almost at random I chose one, looked up his number and dialled him on the automatic exchange. After a long interval a female voice answered me. No, the doctor was out. He had dined with friends to play bridge, he might be back fairly soon. Would I . . . Savagely I cut off and looked up another number. This time the wait seemed an eternity. At last a reply came. 'Do you want Mr Fleming? . . . No, I'm sorry, he's in London till to-morrow.' Would this never end? Miserably it crossed my mind that Maurice, had he come down, would have made no such mistake. He would have called the doctor before the police, and whatever doctor he had called would by a law of nature have been at home. But now at last my third call was answered. 'Yes, it is Mr Kershaw speaking. Yes – yes, good Lord . . . Right. Yes. I'll come at once.' I put down the receiver, and stood waiting anxiously at the gate to meet Dr Kershaw and to take him to the scene of the tragedy.

It must have been about half past ten when I had run down to the Lodge; it was nearly eleven when Kershaw, a young but well-known surgeon who lived at the far end of Holywell, and I joined the little party which had gathered in the Dean's rooms. They stood talking in the outer room when we arrived; an inspector and two policemen, Brendel and Maurice Hargreaves, Pine and, to my surprise, Prendergast and Mitton. Pine, I gathered, had been to their rooms and told them. He felt, apparently, that if a murder had been committed it was the business of our Chaplain and our lawyer to be present, though what they could do was not very obvious to me. Kershaw went straight into the inner room and began to examine the body. The Inspector was obviously appalled by a situation outside his official experience; he glanced at the notes which he had made, and began to question Maurice again about the finding of the body. Meanwhile Brendel in a few brief

47

phrases told me what little had been learned in my absence. Poor Shirley had been shot through the head, probably from a distance of not more than two or three paces; he had apparently been sitting in the arm-chair with his back turned almost, but not quite, towards the murderer. He must, of course, have died instantaneously. Three chambers of the revolver on the table were still loaded; one had just been fired. The bullet had passed through his head, and had lodged in the wall behind the writing-table. The police, assisted by Hargreaves and Brendel himself, had made a searching examination of the rooms, but they had found no trace whatever of the murderer. At first sight, at any rate, it seemed impossible that he could have escaped, for example, by climbing out of one of the back windows. Apart from the fact that there was a sheer drop of some eighteen feet below, he could hardly have got out without leaving some marks. By daylight, no doubt, the police would go over every foot of the ground to confirm or amend this view, but for the time being it seemed almost certain that the murderer must have walked in and out by the ordinary door.

Kershaw's examination did not take long, for the case was only too clear. He could only confirm what we already knew. Suicide, of course, was out of the question. 'If a man shoots himself,' Brendel explained in my ear, 'there is always some charring, because he has to hold the revolver so near to himself. Besides, of course, he couldn't have put the revolver back on the table. He seems to have been shot from a distance of two or three yards; the tiny little hole is where the bullet went in – the other much larger is where it came out. It's just a trifle ragged because of the resistance to its passage inside the head – bone and so forth.'

'How long has he been dead?' asked the Inspector.

'About an hour, perhaps more, perhaps less,' said Kershaw. 'I can't tell more nearly than that.'

48

I saw Brendel make a rapid entry in a little note-book which he had drawn from his pocket.

'That would make it about ten o'clock?' he said.

Kershaw nodded. 'But don't tie me down to any pronouncement of that sort,' he said. 'I think he's been dead about an hour, but that's only a guess, after all.'

Again my mind refused to live up to the situation. I was thinking now only of absurd little details. Ought I to offer a drink to the policemen before they went? Would it be indecent to smoke in that outer room next door to the murdered body? Wherever was Maurice to sleep? The scouts all went out of college to their homes about nine o'clock, and there would be no one to make up a bed for him. But he couldn't sleep, surely, in his bedroom with the corpse lying next door. Should I offer him a shake-down in my own spare room? Ought I to explain to the Inspector who Brendel was and his reputation as an investigator of crime? Or would that be a tactless exposure of something which ought to be kept secret? Round and round in my head went all those stupid questions; more and more I felt certain that whatever I did would certainly be wrong. I felt an almost insane desire to say or do something which would stamp me as a practical man, able to deal with any crisis.

But while I hesitated how to begin, decisions were already being taken.

'We can't do anything more here to-night,' said the Inspector. 'The rooms must be locked up, and I think that the night porter had better keep an eye on them, too. I'll be round first thing in the morning. Have you got a key of the outer room, Sir?'

'I think,' said Maurice, 'that my key's probably in his pocket.' He indicated Shirley's body with a movement of his head.

Rather gingerly, I thought, the Inspector crossed the

49

room and fumbled in the dead man's pocket. He pulled out a key and showed it to Maurice.

'Is that the one?'

'Yes, that's it. Now we had better lock up. But first I'll get a few things for the night from my bedroom.' He seemed now to have recovered his usual habit of command. As he collected pyjamas and shaving tackle from the room within he decided all the questions which had been agitating my mind. 'Francis, you must give me a shake-down in your room for the night. Inspector, you and your men must come down and have something to drink before you leave – and you, too, Kershaw – we all need something pretty stiff after this. The Common Room will still be open, and there are drinks there. Brendel, we shall want your help over this matter. If this isn't a real murder then nothing is.' I felt that the direction of affairs had been assumed by stronger hands than mine.

It was just then that Prendergast spoke, and presented us without warning with a new problem.

'Who,' he said quite suddenly and very quietly, 'who is going to tell Ruth?'

# CHAPTER FIVE

WHEN first I started this chronicle I said that I would tell a plain tale in a straightforward way, nor, in my simplicity, did it occur to me that that would be any very difficult task. And yet what could be harder? For here I have already written four chapters, and still the most important characters have not appeared. What should I say to a pupil who wrote me an essay and never really began to grapple with the subject till his essay was a third done? How easily I should point out the importance of striking at once to the heart of a problem, of fixing the interest of the reader on the main topic, of concentrating upon the essential figures. How easy is criticism, how woefully difficult is construction! How now, at long last, I begin to respect the artist, be his creation never so humble! It is a humiliating confession for me, who all my life have watched and encouraged and criticized, and always with the secret thought that I could easily outshine the writers and the doers if only I cared to make the effort. And now I begin to see that it is not just fastidiousness, not even just idleness which has restrained me, but a lack, a miserable lack, of creative energy and artistic power. Humiliation indeed! I, who in my superior wisdom have lightly criticized so many youthful essays and reviewed so many books, cannot now set a plain tale on paper without hesitations and omissions and turnings back to events that should have been narrated three chapters since. I cannot now start this chronicle again; such as it is it must stand. But at least I must postpone no longer an account of the Verekers – of the President of St Thomas's and his two daughters. For how otherwise could I face old members of the college? They might read a few chapters of this book out of loyalty to their old college, or even out of curiosity, but would they not then throw it impatiently aside?

'Nothing about the Verekers,' they would say, 'but then it's *not* St Thomas's'.' So the effort must be made, however unfitted the author to the task. And first for the bald facts.

Henry Vereker had been elected President of St Thomas's nineteen years before – to be exact, in the glorious warm summer of 1911, and since then he had ruled over us – a courtly, white-haired, gentle, rather frail man, who lived still, as it seemed to most of us, in the more leisured atmosphere of Edwardian, or even of late Victorian times. His wife had been at once a stronger and a finer type. As I remember her, indeed, she had been a remarkable woman, not very artistic, not very clever, and yet, by virtue of character and a deep instinctive sympathy for others, a kind of natural leader; devoted to her family, and adored by them. Other women had a deep respect and liking for her, and, since it was her habit to speak ill of no one, everyone had nothing but good to speak of her. As wife of the Head of one of Oxford's greatest colleges she was happily and fortunately placed, but in 1913, very suddenly, she died, and from that grief the President never quite recovered. He fulfilled his duties, and fulfilled them admirably – no Head of a House was better liked or more generally respected – but his heart was buried in the past. There were two daughters, Ruth who was fourteen when her mother died, and Mary who was four years younger; each of them in turn had filled her mother's place in the President's Lodgings, and each had filled it to admiration.

Ruth and Mary. How can I describe them? I guess well enough how some of the great artists might have painted them; I can imagine how some of my favourite poets might have pictured their charm; most clearly of all I can see them illuminating the pages of George Meredith. But I am an old bachelor of sixty. If anything here is lacking to them of youthful charms and womanly allure, blame me, not them.

It is the fashion among men of my generation when they wish to bestow the highest praise on a young woman to say, 'Thank God, she isn't one of those modern, cocktail-drinking, cigarette-smoking, jazzing modern creatures.' It would be true to say that of Ruth and Mary, and yet it would be only a fraction of the truth. For they were both children of their own post-war generation, though they escaped, as it seemed naturally, its less attractive traits ... The secret, as I believe, of their charm was an intense enjoyment of life, and a love and comprehensive sympathy for the lives of others. If you had tea with Ruth you knew that she would rejoice with you in your minor triumphs, and sympathize with understanding in your petty disappointments; if you took Mary to the theatre you knew before you started that she as well as you would enjoy every moment of the evening. Like Lady Everingham in *Coningsby*, they possessed the two fine qualities which make the art of conversation. They could originate, and they could sympathize, for they possessed at the same time 'the habit of communicating and the habit of listening.' They had inherited their character and their sympathy from their mother, their charm of manner and their good looks from their father. They seemed, too, to exercise their sway over callow undergraduates and middle-aged dons with equal facility. How often in their drawing-room had I seen a crusty professor thaw and become youthful and enthusiastic, or a shy and tongue-tied undergraduate cast aside his stiff and clumsy mannerisms to grow gay, and natural and happy. It used to be a saying in the years after the war that every undergraduate at St Thomas's was in love with one of the Verekers, and every don with both. It pleased me, as a confirmed bachelor, to suppose that my affection for them was of a semi-paternal kind. Perhaps it was – I cannot be quite sure. But I am certain that of all the young ladies whom I have met none could hold a candle to Ruth and Mary

Vereker. I know I am a sentimentalist, but where they are concerned, who could be otherwise? They had, of course, been brought up in college and I think they loved St Thomas's and all that belonged to it almost as much as St Thomas's loved them.

It was in 1927 that Ruth married. I can still feel the shock which the announcement of her engagement gave me. Men, I remember to have thought, are difficult to understand, but women are impossible. For with all Oxford at her feet, Ruth must needs become engaged to Shirley. Shirley, who of us all was least sociable and most forbidding, who went less often than any to the President's Lodgings, who more than any of us was harshly intolerant of women, who went out of his way to scarify their intelligence and their influence. They fell in love with one another; no amount of words could explain it further. I think when he married that Shirley made an honest effort to curb his tongue and modify the bitterness of his nature. When his wife was present he was a gentler and more human person; at least I never heard him address to her one of those caustic remarks from which in male society he could never for long abstain. But it is difficult at forty-five to alter the habits of a lifetime. I hoped that he might mellow, but I was disappointed. A failure in 1928 to secure appointment to a Professorship which he had long coveted left him as bitterly disgruntled and as uncompromisingly sarcastic as he had been before his marriage. Ruth felt her husband's unpopularity deeply, though she hid her feelings from the world. She made heroic efforts to soften him, and to make him take pleasure in society. Herself the most happy-natured and companionable of people, she suffered intensely as she saw that Shirley was shunned and disliked by almost all who came in contact with him. We all tried to help her but help was really impossible. Young men, who, for Ruth's sake, had lunched or dined at her house, would almost invariably be the victims of some mordant sarcasm from their host – a sarcasm which bit the deeper because it was almost invariably based on a fiendishly accurate insight into character. And so, though she put a brave face on it, Ruth knew, as we knew, that she had failed. Yet she loved Shirley, and in some curious, to me incomprehensible, way I believe that she was happy.

When Ruth married, Mary took over the care and management of her father's house. She was then twenty-four, and in the full flush of her beauty. A little quieter than her sister, a little harder to know at first, yet she had the same sunny disposition, the same irresistible charm. Yes, irresistible is the word; where she was seen, there she conquered. With her as hostess, the President's Lodgings continued to be the centre of college life. We all went there, dons and undergraduates alike – not out of any sense of college duty, but because we liked to go, because Mary would be there to welcome us, to cheer us, to make us feel that the world in general, and St Thomas's in particular, was a good and a cheerful and a happy place.

It was in autumn of 1929 that *The Times* announced the second impending blow as it had announced the first. Mary, so I read on one ill-fated morning, was engaged to Maurice Hargreaves. I confess that I was profoundly and irrationally annoyed. In many ways the engagement was in the highest degree suitable. Maurice had a comfortable income of his own, he was handsome, popular, and distinguished in his own sphere. Moreover he was a dominant personality at St Thomas's, with strong claims to succeed Henry Vereker as President when the time for a change should come. And yet I hated the thought of that engagement. I told myself that Maurice was too old, though he was after all only forty; I remembered that he had the reputation of being something too much of a ladies' man in the worse sense of that term. But really, I think, I hated the thought of his early success. Why should everything fall into his lap? He had conquered too easily the worlds of scholarship and sport, and now it seemed he had only to hold out his hand and beckon to him the best and kindest of women. The man's everlasting success alienated all my sympathy from him. Did he realize, was he sufficiently thankful for all his good fortune? For me, though I struggled to subdue the thought, he became the symbol of success too easily won, too obviously expected. I thought that he suffered from ὕβρις, I longed in spite of myself to see him in some way chastened and humbled. I don't excuse my own attitude, I only chronicle it. For the first time I admitted to myself what I had long known subconsciously, but carefully concealed. I did not really like Maurice, I envied him, I was jealous. Three months now had passed since the engagement had been announced; they were to be married in the summer.

*

When Prendergast asked his question we all looked at one another uncomfortably. Shirley had been to most of us so inhuman that his sudden end seemed, I believe, to each of us like an event outside our own lives. Prendergast told me afterwards that when first he saw him lying there dead it seemed to him, after the first shock had passed, like a problem in crime set before him for solution. But the moment that Ruth's name was mentioned everything was changed. It ceased to be a problem and became a human tragedy, with which we had to deal. Who was to tell Ruth? It was no pleasant task, yet clearly it had to be done. She expected her husband back that night in North Oxford, she might not improbably be sitting up for him; she could not be left in ignorance till the morning. As usual I hesitated and wavered. I was the oldest man there, I knew her better than did any of the others; was it my duty, I wondered, to proffer my services? I was rescued from my doubts by little

56

Mitton. I had never thought very highly of our Chaplain, but at that moment I admired his courage.

'That's my job, I think,' he said, and began to button up his coat. I realized dimly that even if he might at times cut a rather foolish figure he had underneath that a real belief in the dignity of his cloth and a belief in his calling. I respected him as I had never done before. The others agreed, and Mitton prepared to set off on his gloomy errand. 'Don't let her come down to-night whatever you do,' said Maurice. 'She can do no good, and it's too ghastly to think of her seeing him like this here in the middle of the night. We won't tell the President and Mary till to-morrow. It can't be right to wake them all up now. God knows it'll be bad enough for them in the morning.'

I was thankful for that decision, for I felt that my nerves would stand no more that evening. We locked up first the inner room, and then the oak, and took our way back to the empty Common Room. Only three hours before in that same place Brendel had theorized on murder and the detection of crime. As we entered the room I heard him mutter to himself; it sounded as though he said, 'I am very much to blame.'

# CHAPTER SIX

IN retrospect the next morning appears to me as a prolonged and loathsome nightmare. Bad news travels quickly, and, when I got up after a feverish and miserable night, it seemed as though everyone knew already of the tragedy of the evening before. I was torn from my academic calm and plunged into a world which was utterly new and strange to me. I spent an hour assisting Maurice in making practical arrangements, in interviewing the police, in agreeing with them on a brief and non-committal statement for the press, in cancelling the various engagements with pupils that I had for that day. Never till then had I realized how sheltered my life had always been; how everything had been done decently and in order; and how unfitted I was for dealing with a harder and less academic world. In the middle of the morning came the summons which I had both expected and dreaded. 'The President's compliments and would Mr Winn call upon him as soon as he conveniently could.' I put on my gown and walked to the President's Lodgings.

I knew well enough before I entered that the President would take the news hardly. Since his wife had died he had had two great interests in his life – his daughters and the college. Now both the things that he loved best were stricken at the same time. He loved the college with the devotion of a man who had dedicated to its interests all his life and energies, but his affection was of a fastidious and discriminating kind. Above anything else he hated vulgarity and advertisement, and, though no one was prouder than he if St Thomas's men distinguished themselves in the schools or on the playing-fields, yet he hated to see such successes paraded in the daily press. Mention of the college he could tolerate if it took the form of allusion to our great traditions, our noble buildings, our historic names. An account of this kind if couched in the choicest eighteenth-century Johnsonian prose might even give him pleasure. But if, for example, one of our undergraduates was fined for some trivial motoring offence, and the words 'undergraduate at St Thomas's College, Oxford,' appeared in the paper after his name, the President would feel that he had been personally insulted. In all our long acquaintance I had only once seen him really angry, and that was when a well-meaning but injudicious friend had sent him a cutting from an Australian paper in which a returned Rhodes scholar had written an account, accurate enough, but perhaps a little too blatantly appreciative, of the life and personnel of St Thomas's. The happiest moment of the President's life had been, I think, when a guest one night at dinner had said to him, 'President, I think that St Thomas's is the best college at Oxford, and talks about it least.' And now this courtly old gentleman, who all his life had shrunk from contact with the world, was faced with the horrible publicity of a murder inside his own college, and that the murder of his own son-in-law in the rooms of another son-in-law to be. No Grand Inquisitor could have devised for him a more refined form of slow torture. In my mind's eye I saw the headlines in the papers for the next few days, and I saw, too, the poor old man's face as he read them.

My interview with him was painful, and I will not dwell on it. 'This is a dreadful thing for the college, and for my poor daughter.' That was the burden of his cry, and I could do or say nothing to help. I could only tell him all that I knew of the crime, and of the investigations of the Oxford police. They had found, so I had been told, no clue of any kind, and had no theory to explain the murder. With commendable promptitude they had decided that the best assistance available was needed and they had already telephoned to London. Inspector Cotter, from Scotland Yard, was to arrive by the two o'clock train. I promised to report any new developments and took my leave.

As I went out I met Mary; she must have been waiting for me in the hall. 'Mr Winn,' she exclaimed, 'this is terrible. I can't understand it. It all seems so horrible and so unreal. Who could wish to shoot him, and in Maurice's rooms?' I saw that she was overwrought, and tried to pacify her as best I could.

'Mary,' I said, 'your first duty is to Ruth. You must keep calm, if only to help her. I suppose she has come down here?'

'Poor Ruth! Yes, she has come home for the time being. Of course I'll do my best to help. But, Mr Winn, we must find out the truth about this wicked murder. It's the mystery which makes it so hideous. Promise me that you'll find out.'

I had never refused a request from Mary in my life, and I could not now.

'Yes, Mary,' I said, 'I promise you I'll find out. Now, good-bye.'

How I was to fulfil my promise I had not the remotest idea, but somewhere in the back of my mind I had a child-like faith in Brendel. If any man could get at the truth, surely it was he.

*

Shortly after two o'clock Inspector Cotter arrived. Anyone less like the detective of fiction it would be impossible to imagine; to me, alike in dress and manner and personal appearance he seemed to be the embodiment of the average man. Only his eyes were out of the ordinary, for they were keen and intelligent. It was soon clear that the Inspector, even if he lacked the appearance of a man of parts, was no sluggard at his work. He examined every detail of the Dean's rooms, exploring, measuring, noting. Then one by one he questioned those of us who had been present on the previous evening.

He made no attempt to hurry, and no attempt to force an answer, yet question followed question with relentless relevance. Every fact which could have any bearing on the tragedy was elicited in its turn and duly tabulated. I had always flattered myself that I knew how to conduct a viva voce examination; when I watched Inspector Cotter at work, I realized that I had not learned the rudiments of the art of inquiry.

'A competent chap, that,' said the Bursar appreciatively after a quarter of an hour's interview. 'He asks all the right questions, and notes down all the answers.' The Bursar certainly thought that the expert had given official approval to his own favourite methods. Only Maurice Hargreaves, after a prolonged *tête-à-tête*, emerged, flushed and slightly angry. I took some pleasure in reflecting that he had in all probability found it hard to explain exactly why he had left a loaded revolver lying on the table in his room.

At six o'clock Cotter came back to my rooms, and asked if he might talk to me again. I acquiesced, of course, and settled him into an arm-chair by my fire. I was gratified to find that he had no affectation of mystery or secrecy, nor did he attempt to hint at any clues which his examination had revealed. He seemed anxious only to arrive at the truth, and keen to avail himself of any help which he could get.

'Mr Winn,' he said, 'I've seen all that I can, and I think I've spoken to everyone who might be able to throw any light on this affair. Now I want to ask you some more questions, and I hope you'll be able to answer them.'

He paused, and looked at me as though asking a question. 'Go on,' I said. 'I see no reason at all why I should not give you a perfectly straightforward answer to any question which you can ask.'

'Thank you. But before I begin there are certain facts which you ought to know.'

He paused again, this time to give weight to what he had to say, then he continued.

'Mr Winn, this was a callous and brutal murder. That is the one fact of which I am convinced. No other explanation is tenable. The revolver has been carefully examined for finger-prints and this is the result: the murderer, whoever he was, most certainly wore gloves. You don't wear gloves in a gentleman's room in Oxford except for a purpose, do you?'

Again he paused to let this fact sink into my mind. Then he went on rather bitterly. 'And that, Mr Winn, is the only fact that we have got to help us. We know that Mr Shirley was shot, we know that the murderer remembered to put on gloves to shoot him, we know that he used the revolver in the room to do it with; we know, from what Dr Kershaw says, that he did it round about ten o'clock – let's say to be safe between nine-fifteen and ten minutes past ten, when you went up to the room. Beyond that we've got nothing – nothing whatever. You see,' his tone was almost resentful, 'a hundred people a day would go up to that room to see Mr Hargreaves about one thing or another, and no one would pay any attention to them. A Dean seems to be a busy person in this place. And of course no one noticed the shot, with all those young idiots letting off fireworks and shouting about down below. It couldn't be more unlucky. There isn't a damned clue anywhere. But I'll get him all the same.'

He fixed his eyes on me. 'And now, Sir, perhaps you'll be very kind and let me fire off some questions at you?'

'Carry on,' I replied, 'I'm quite ready.'

'First of all I want to be quite sure about strangers getting into this college after dark. Your porter told me about the arrangements, but I want to be quite sure I've got it right.'

"That's quite simple,' I said. 'The gates are shut and locked every evening at nine o'clock. After that everyone who comes in has to give his name. The Head Porter, or one of the under porters, sits in the lodge and opens the gate, and enters the names in a book. You can see the book if you like and check up the entries. Undergraduates pay a small fee on their battels for coming in after a certain time. I forget exactly what it is, but I know that it is increased if they come in after eleven. After twelve they can't come in at all except with special leave, and there's no one at the gate – but of course that doesn't affect the matter.'

'And there's no way in except through the lodge?'

'Oh, yes, there is. There's an entrance by the kitchen, locked up when the chef and the staff go home, I suppose about nine o'clock, and there are two small entrances, one in the back Quad, and one at the bottom of the staircase where Mr Hargreaves' rooms are, but they can only be opened by private keys.'

'Who has got keys to them?'

'All the Fellows, and I think, the Head Porter. We use the entrance on the Dean's staircase a good deal. It's generally called the Fellows' door.'

'Couldn't anyone else have one of these keys?'

'I don't think so. You see we keep them pretty carefully. It wouldn't do at all if an undergraduate, for instance, got hold of a private key into the place. Once every term the Bursar sends round a note to ask each of us if our pass key is safely in our possession. Once someone lost his, and we had all the locks and keys changed for security.'

'Are there any other ways in at all?'

I smiled. 'I'm led to believe that it's possible to climb in, but some of the undergraduates know more about that than I do. I don't think it's very easy. If it's important I expect that I could find one of them to show you the popular routes.' As I spoke my thoughts turned to Scarborough and Garnett.

'I don't think we need trouble about that; not yet anyhow. It amounts to this then. There's a very strong presumption that the murderer, whoever he was, was in the college before the gates were shut at nine o'clock.'

I agreed; any other conclusion seemed highly improbable.

I expected that Cotter would turn to some other aspect of the case, but I was wrong. He still seemed hardly satisfied, and he now produced from his pocket a plan of St Thomas's and laid it before me.

'I don't want to be tiresome,' he said half apologetically, 'but I'd be obliged if you'd glance at that plan and show me just where these different entrances are; and while you're doing that perhaps you'd make quite sure that you've not missed out any of the ways in. In my profession we can't leave anything to chance.'

I could not help feeling a little irritated at his request. It was not really credible that after living for forty years in the college I should forget one of the gates. However I could not well refuse his request, so I took up the plan and proceeded to enlighten him.

'Here is the main gate at the south side of the large Quadrangle, and here, on the opposite side, is what I called the Fellows' door. And here . . . Oh, good gracious, there *is* another way in that I had quite forgotten.'

Cotter made a very praiseworthy attempt to conceal his smile.

'It's the President's Lodgings,' I explained. 'Of course I never thought of that. You see the President's House, or Lodgings as we call it, forms the greater part of the eastern side of the smaller Quadrangle. It has a front door and a back door both opening into the garden, and so into the street, and another door – a second front door you might almost call it – which gives access to the Quadrangle. But it's really of very little consequence, for no one in the house would be likely to use it at that time of night.'

64

'Still, I should like to know who would be in the house at that time.'

'The President and his daughter, Miss Vereker, the butler and three or four maidservants. Oh, and an old friend of the President's and his wife. I remember that because it was the reason why the President wanted Professor Brendel to stay in college rather than with him. He always prefers to be able to devote himself to one guest at a time.'

Cotter made a brief entry in his note-book, and then continued his interrogatory.

'Did anybody stand to gain by Mr Shirley's death – financially, I mean, or in any way like that?'

'I don't think so; he was a poor man – I doubt if he had any money to speak of outside what he earned. His wife had a few hundreds a year from her mother, but even so they were by no means well off. No, I can't think that anyone could benefit in that sort of way from his death.'

Cotter paused again before his next question, and his tone when he continued was fairly apologetic.

'I put some of these questions to the President,' he said, 'because I understood that he was the father-in-law, but he didn't seemed disposed to tell me anything.'

I smiled again. It was not difficult for me to imagine the frosty though courteous determination with which the poor old President would decline to discuss his private affairs with a detective.

'Never mind,' I said, 'I'll try to repair the omissions.'

'Well, was Mr Shirley quite happy in his family life?'

'Yes, I think so far as a man of his temperament could be happy he was. Certainly there had never been the hint of a quarrel between him and his wife.'

'Hm. Good. And had he any enemies in the college?'

That was a more difficult question, and I hesitated for a time before I answered.

65

'Well,' I said at last, 'the fact is, Inspector, that Shirley was a very unpopular man. It's no good my trying to conceal that fact from you, even if I wished to. He had hardly any friends, except perhaps Mottram, and a good many enemies. Most members of Common Room used to avoid sitting next to him if they could.'

The Inspector's interest was visibly aroused.

'That might be important,' he said. 'Was there anyone with whom he had any special quarrel?'

I began to wish that I had not spoken quite so definitely, but there was no going back now.

'Yes, he had quarrelled openly, I'm afraid, with Shepardson. He had written some rather nasty things about Shepardson's book, and they hadn't been on speaking terms for the last month or two. But for Heaven's sake don't get a wrong impression. Men don't shoot one another because of literary disagreements, however bitter they may have been in print.'

'Perhaps not, but we can't afford to neglect any point, however unpromising. Was this Mr Shepardson at dinner last night?'

'Yes.'

'And you had some sort of a discussion about murder, so they tell me, started by this Professor Brendel. Now who exactly is he?'

I explained to him the reasons for Brendel's visit, and told him what I remembered of the discussion.

'Yes, I believe I've heard of Brendel not so long ago,' he said thoughtfully. 'One of our men was out in Vienna and ran into him there. If what he told me is true your Professor Brendel can see further through a haystack than most.'

He pocketed his notes and stood up.

'Well, I mustn't keep you any longer,' he said. 'I think I'll go and see the porter who was on duty at the lodge last night, and I'd like to have a bit of a talk with this

Professor Brendel. But it's a fair puzzle, however you look at it. Good night, Sir, and thank you.'

He went out, and I decided that it was time for me to dress for dinner.

# CHAPTER SEVEN

WE were a largish party at dinner that night, for everyone was anxious to hear what the police investigations had elicited. Even two of my married colleagues, who seldom deserted their homes in North Oxford except on Sunday evenings, and a professor who was attached to St Thomas's, had been driven by curiosity to put their names on the list for dinner that night. I had not seen Brendel all day. He had given the first of his lectures that afternoon, and had therefore had little time to spare. He gave me a friendly greeting as we went into Hall, but I thought he looked tired and harassed.

By tacit agreement we kept off the subject which filled all our minds so long as we were in Hall – it seemed better not to discuss it before the servants – but as soon as we were settled in our places in Common Room an eager debate began. It would have taken more than a murder to repress John Doyne's spirits for long, and his first question to me was almost flippant.

'What has the official sleuth discovered, Winn?' he said. 'He was closeted with you for the best part of an hour. Is he going to arrest you in the morning for murdering one of your colleagues.'

'Really, John,' I protested, 'you mustn't talk like that. No. Inspector Cotter seems to be utterly fogged. There is one thing though, but please don't mention it outside this room. They've discovered that the murderer put on gloves, so he must have planned the whole thing in a filthy cold-blooded way. Beyond that they've discovered nothing at all. The Inspector says that there simply isn't a clue of any kind. But they're working hard, and leaving no stone unturned.'

My information produced an immense and immediate sensation.

'That's awful,' said Dixon. 'The brute must have worked the whole thing out, and shot him down like a dog.'

'But Sherlock Cotter is leaving no stone unturned,' said the irrepressible Doyne. 'I suppose that, in detective circles, is the same as what the politicians call exploring every avenue. That means in this country, you know' (he turned to Brendel), 'that they haven't the foggiest idea what to do, and are just waiting for something to turn up. Couldn't we help Cotter; we all know the facts, and are, as we all admit, an exceedingly intelligent set of men. What's your theory, Winn?'

'I'm afraid I haven't the remotest idea,' I answered. 'The whole thing is utterly mystifying. How can anyone explain a murder when there's no clue, and no motive for the murder?'

'Ah, the truth is you've no imagination,' said Doyne. 'But I have, and my theory is this. You all remember Maurice's story last night about Fothergill murdering his scout and burying him in the meadow. I believe that this is the second chapter of that old story. Fate working out its inexorable revenge. Somewhere in the scout subconsciousness, you know, there has always been a desire to right that ancient wrong. The vendetta has been handed down from scout to scout, and this is the result. Probably Shirley's scout, day after day for twenty years, heard him complain of his breakfast until at last he could bear it no longer, and shot him through the head. How's that for an explanation?'

'Ingenious, John, but manifestly fallacious,' said Whitaker. 'To begin with Shirley has breakfasted for the last three years at home in North Oxford, and Crossett who used to be his scout in college died last year. My explanation is much simpler. Some undergraduate who had felt the heavy hand of the Dean, arrived to shoot him; the Dean was not at home, so rather than waste an opportunity

69

he shot Shirley instead, and then cleared out. How about that?'

'Equally impossible,' returned Doyne, 'the motive is inadequate, and no undergraduate would put on his gloves to shoot the Dean. You must try again.'

Mitton had been growing visibly agitated as the conversation proceeded, and now he turned a bright pink and uttered a not unreasonable protest.

'For pity's sake stop talking like this about it,' he blurted out. 'Shirley has not been dead for twenty-four hours, and you can jest about it. You've no business to speak like this about a sacred subject. Surely the whole thing is clear enough. This is, after all, a Christian College, and it is inconceivable that anyone here could have done such an act. The murder must have been the work of a homicidal maniac. He must have hidden himself in the room and waited for poor Shirley there.'

'Padre, Padre,' interrupted Doyne, 'you must control your language. How can you speak of the murder of a colleague as a sacred subject. It's really not decent. Besides your theory is ludicrously inadequate. Did Providence inform your homicidal maniac that there would be a revolver waiting for him to use in the Dean's rooms? And did he, when he had finished his shooting, climb out of college over the chapel roof, or did he wait all night hidden in some forgotten corner? Really, I'm disappointed at your efforts to help. I don't think you're really trying.'

Mitton's pink had turned to scarlet, and he was preparing to turn on his tormentor, but the Bursar intervened.

'You're all off the track,' he said with military bluntness. 'In affairs like this the obvious solution is usually forgotten, and is nearly always the right one. In this case what happened, I take it, was this. Scarborough and Garnett, who are a pair of rascals anyhow, went up to the Dean's rooms to see whether they could recover their damned revolver. They were probably both drunk, and one of them picked it up and fired it off. Of course they're out of their minds with fright, and ready to deny everything. But if this Inspector, who seems to know his job, and I put a few searching questions to them to-morrow they'll soon spit out the whole story. I'm sorry for the poor young devils; it's a terrible punishment for taking a drink too many.'

'Major,' said Doyne, 'you're worse than the Padre. You don't use your brains at all. Every single bit of evidence is against you. Scarborough's the son of a country squire, and had been brought up with firearms all his life. He might be drunk, but he'd never point a firearm at anyone, whether it was loaded or not. You can't get rid of early training. As for Garnett, all the drink in this college would not, in my humble opinion, make that young gentleman even three parts intoxicated. Besides, by no stretch of imagination can you suppose that Scarborough or Garnett would have put on a pair of gloves in order to ask the Dean to return them their revolver. Hopeless, Major, quite hopeless. But come, Professor, what do you think? This is your special subject, and you ought to be able to help us.'

I was amazed, as we all turned towards Brendel, to observe his embarrassment and distress. He even seemed, as he replied, to have lost temporarily his command of English. He stammered, and spoke in curiously stiff un-English sentences.

'Excuse me, please, excuse me,' he said. 'I . . . I am here a guest. I can in this affair take no part. I have no theory to offer to you.'

'But I have.' Prendergast had taken no part in the discussion, though he had listened with rapt attention. Now his voice rang through the room with a new note of decision and challenge. He hit the table with his clenched fist as he spoke.

'Keep these facts in your minds. Shirley was shot by a man in gloves. Very well, the murder was with intention. He was shot with a revolver which Maurice had left on the table. Who knew that Shirley was in Maurice's rooms? Who knew also that there was a loaded revolver in those rooms? Everyone who was dining here last night, and – in all human probability – no other human soul. Is that your conclusion, too, Professor?'

He stopped abruptly, while his words sank in.

Brendel made a gesture, half of resignation, half of agreement, but when he spoke his words were almost an admission that he shared Prendergast's view.

'No, no,' he said, 'it is not certain. Your butler who waits on us – he may have heard Mr Shirley say that he would wait in the Dean's rooms; he may, too, have heard us speak of the revolver. It is not certain, indeed it is not.'

I got up from my chair and rang the bell. Callendar came in and stood in front of me.

'Callendar,' I said, 'did you hear us speak last night of the revolver in Mr Hargreaves' room?'

'Yes, Sir, in Hall before you came down to Common Room.'

'Were you in the room when Mr Shirley said that he would go up to Mr Hargreaves' rooms?'

'Yes, Sir, I was just putting out the whisky and soda on the side table before I went away.'

'And did you tell anyone else that Mr Shirley had gone there?'

This time it seemed to me that there was a perceptible pause before he replied, but his answer when it came was clear enough.

'No, Sir, I had no reason to, Sir.'

'Thank you, Callendar, that is all,' I said, and he left us.

There was an awkward silence, and then Doyne took the bull by the horns.

'There's something in what you say, Prendergast,' he said at length. 'At any rate,' he added drily, 'it's an avenue which we have got to explore. We can at any rate see which of us deserve to be on the list of suspects. How many dined last night, Winn?'

'Thirteen,' I said, 'including Shirley, but Brendel and I were here together in Common Room until Maurice came back and told us of the murder.'

'That leaves ten,' said Doyne; 'now, Dixon, what about you?'

'I'm safe, too,' said Dixon. 'I went out with Whitaker and Whitaker's guest – Tweddle of Balliol – we let Tweddle out of college and then sat talking in Whitaker's rooms till nearly midnight.'

'Then that disposes of you three.'

'No, by Jove, it doesn't,' said Whitaker. 'Tweddle came back ten minutes after he left to say that he had left a scarf behind, as indeed he had. That must have been just before ten.'

'So he was in college again for five minutes on his own,' said Doyne. 'Just long enough to do the business.'

'Yes, but hang it all,' protested Whitaker, 'I don't suppose he knew Shirley from Adam. You really can't imagine that he did it.'

'A scientist from Balliol might do anything,' said Doyne judicially. 'Besides, Shirley had probably insulted him at least once at dinner. Anyhow, he goes down on the list of suspects. Shepardson, you're next.'

'I had two pupils, Howe and Martin; they were with me till after ten, I know. I can't remember the exact time. After that I read a novel, and then I went to bed.'

'A doubtful case,' said Doyne. 'If you were quick you had time to do it after Howe and Martin left you, but only just. I fancy that you're almost entitled to the benefit of the doubt, but not quite. I shall have to put you among the

73

suspects, at least until the evidence of Howe and Martin has been taken. Your turn, Bursar.'

'I went out with Mitton – I forget just when. I meant to look over some accounts, but as a matter of fact I went to sleep in my chair, and didn't wake up until it was time to go to bed.'

'Highly suspicious, Major, especially for a man whose profession was so long one of legalized slaughter. You join the suspects.'

Trower, I could see, did not like the pleasantry, but he said nothing, and Doyne turned to Mitton.

'Well, Mitt?'

The Chaplain blushed even more fiercely than ever. 'I went straight to my rooms,' he said, 'and you know I don't sleep very well when I've had a glass of port, so I sat down and played patience for an hour or more to calm my nerves before bedtime.'

'Lamentable!' exclaimed Doyne. 'The grown male who will play a lonely game of patience might murder anyone. Your name heads the list of suspects. Who else was dining, Winn?'

I did not at all like the trend of the conversation, but, having gone so far, it was impossible to turn back. 'Hargreaves, Mottram, Prendergast and yourself,' I said.

Doyne thought a moment, then smiled rather wryly.

'I'm afraid you must go on the list, Maurice; you found him and therefore you could have shot him. Now, Mottram?'

Mottram looked dreadfully ill and haggard, and I felt sorry for him. He was the only one there who could fairly be described as a friend of the dead man's, and I began to think that the murder, coming on top of his own disappointment with his work, had been too much for him. But he answered readily enough.

'I drove up to the Lab. in my car, about nine o'clock,

I suppose, and worked there most of the evening. Let me see. One of the demonstrators from next door came in to see me just after I arrived, and Holt of Magdalen, who has the room opposite, and who was working late, came in for a cigarette just after ten. Otherwise I was alone. I came back to bed between twelve and one, and left the car for the night outside college.'

'That's clear enough,' said Doyne, 'but even you aren't quite safe. With your car you could have come down to college and gone back again to the Lab. in a quarter of an hour. You're on the list, too.'

Prendergast's turn came next.

'I went out of Common Room as you know at ten o'clock,' he said. 'I had a pupil to whom I'd promised to lend some books then. I waited for him, but for some reason he never came. I thought it was too late to come back to Common Room, so I worked at some notes for my lecture to-day until Pine came running up and told me what had happened.'

Doyne whistled. 'You're as bad as the rest,' he said. 'Not a soul to answer for you just at the critical time.'

'And what about yourself, John?' asked Prendergast.

'Let me see,' said Doyne. 'I went out of Common Room when Pine told us that there was a noise going on in the Quad – about a quarter to ten, I suppose. I waited for a bit in the front Quad, and then I strolled into the back Quad, to see if things were all right there. I found that most of the young men had retired to their rooms – there was a good deal of noise, but no harm being done. I was just coming back when I saw Polson – the stroke of the second togger – in an advanced state of intoxication. He was in fact extremely tight, and his friends seemed to have temporarily deserted him. He's a nice lad really, and I didn't want him to get into any trouble, so I thought I'd take him to his rooms. I did that, and a pretty tough job it was. Having got him there I thought I'd better see him safely into bed, so I did that, too. No boy's job either.'

He paused and looked round. 'Good Lord,' he said, 'I'm in the worst position of the lot. The only witness to my innocence is an undergraduate who was much too drunk to remember seeing me at all. I'll have to bracket myself with Mitt at the top of the suspects' list.'

'But this is fantastic,' said Prendergast. 'I never heard of such a rotten set of alibis. Twelve of us dined with Shirley last night, and of those eight, if you include this Tweddle creature from Balliol, haven't a shadow of proof of their innocence. It's fantastic, I say.'

'The whole thing is fantastic,' said Dixon. 'Shirley is murdered without rhyme or reason; the murderer leaves no trace whatever, and eight men of unblemished reputation are found by your infernal deductions to contain among them a brutal and accomplished murderer. Are we all quite sane?'

'For heaven's sake don't let us lose our heads,' I cried. 'This affair is getting on our nerves. I don't believe for a single instant that anyone who dined last night killed Shirley, however convincing Prendergast's arguments may sound. But we *must* find out who the murderer was. If we don't, life here will be intolerable for us all; we'll be left with a hideous suspicion that one of those eight did it. It'll poison our whole lives. We can't go on like that. Brendel,' I said, turning to him almost savagely, 'you *must* help us. You can't refuse now. Think what our position is if this crime remains a mystery! For heaven's sake say you will help.'

He made a deprecatory movement with his hand.

'I don't know whether I can help, but, yes, I must try. I was afraid that you would say that, and it's true enough. Yes. I'll try to find the murderer for you, but listen.' His voice became very grave as he spoke. 'I am afraid, I am terribly afraid, of what I shall find.'

76

We did not stay much longer in Common Room after that. Everyone was ill at ease, and I was glad enough to make an excuse to get away. Brendel had intimated to me that there were questions which he wished to ask me, and I suggested that there was no time for them like the present. As we walked out into the Quad, a figure stepped out of the shadow, and accosted me. It was Callendar.

'May I have a word with you, Sir?' he said.

'Of course, come up to my rooms now.'

Brendel looked keenly at him, and then, rather to my surprise, walked with us to my rooms. We went in, and I told Callendar to tell me what he wanted.

'If you please, Sir,' he said, 'what I have to say is private.'

A quick nod from Brendel gave me my cue.

'If it has to do with the murder, Callendar, I hope that you will not mind speaking in Professor Brendel's presence. The Professor is going to help us to investigate the affair.'

The butler looked at Brendel, and was apparently satisfied. I noticed once again the odd power which the latter had of inspiring confidence even in men whom he met for the first time.

'Very well, Sir,' said Callendar, 'if those are your wishes.'

He seemed to pull himself together as though for an effort, and then continued.

'When you asked me just now, Sir, if I had told anyone that Mr Shirley had gone to the Dean's rooms last night I said I hadn't. Well, Sir, it wasn't true. I had.'

'Whom did you tell, Callendar?' I asked.

'Mr Scarborough, Sir,' replied the butler.

# CHAPTER EIGHT

I HAD had many shocks that evening, but in some ways this was the most unexpected and the most alarming of them all. When Callendar had begun to unburden himself I had been conscious of a sudden lightening of anxiety, a sense of impending freedom from fear. As he told us that after all another besides ourselves had known of Shirley's movements, the whole fabric of suspicion against the 'suspects' had appeared to collapse. I had breathed for a moment freely again. And now one anxiety was replaced by a still graver one. Scarborough, for whose conduct and well-being I had some personal responsibility, was directly and dangerously under suspicion. I made an effort to appear at my ease, and steadied my voice to ask Callendar some further questions.

'How did that happen, Callendar?'

'It was like this, Sir. I'd just finished in Common Room, round about nine-fifteen as usual, and I came out of my pantry on my way to go home. And there was Mr Scarborough waiting in the Quad, and that there Mr Garnett with him. "Good evening, Callendar," he says. He was always friendly to me, for I was scout, you know, Sir, to his father thirty years ago. "Good evening, Sir," I said. "Has Mr Shirley gone up to his room yet, Callendar? I want to catch him as he comes out." "No, Sir," I said, "but he's gone up to the Dean's room to wait for Mr Hargreaves there." "You can't chase him up there, Scar," says Mr Garnett. "No, damn and blast him" (if you'll excuse me, Sir), says Mr Scarborough.'

'Did they say anything else after that?'

'Yes, Sir, they did. They used some language about Mr Shirley not at all suitable to repeat.'

'What did they say?'

'I can't repeat what they said, Sir, it wasn't suitable, especially about a gentleman that's dead.'

'But you may have to at the inquest or later on,' I said rather injudiciously.

'Begging your pardon, Sir, I'll do nothing of the sort. I know what's proper words to use and what aren't.'

I did not press the question; I was uncomfortably sure that Scarborough's language about his tutor had been even more violent than usual.

'Was there anything more?' I said.

'Yes, Sir, Mr Garnett said, "I suppose he'll be shown our revolver up there when the Dean goes up," and Mr Scarborough said, vindictive like, "I only wish someone would shoot him with it." And then they said "Good night," and I went home. But I didn't like to say too much about it all when you asked me in Common Room, Sir, considering all that's happened.'

'You did quite right, Callendar. Better not speak to anyone else about this, for the present anyhow.'

'Not even to that Scotland Yard Inspector, Sir, that was asking me all those questions this afternoon?'

'No,' I said, with a decision which is unusual to me. 'You have told me and that is sufficient. Good night, Callendar, and thank you.'

As the door closed behind the butler I noticed that all the little wrinkles round Brendel's eyes were showing in a smile which he could not suppress.

'You seem to have begun very early to conceal information from the police,' he observed; 'that's quite according to the tradition of detective fiction.'

I had the grace to feel faintly ashamed of myself.

'Perhaps I ought not to have done that,' I said, 'but it's frightening me. Every hour some new possibility seems to appear, and it's always something worse than before. This boy's father regards me as more or less responsible for his son, and it now seems that of everyone mixed up in this wretched affair he's in the most danger.'

Brendel saw that I was really alarmed, and he patted me on the shoulder, as though to restore my confidence.

'Don't be alarmed, my friend,' he said. 'We can build too much on a coincidence of this kind. We may find that your protégé, whose language is so fierce, wanted to speak to Shirley for some quite innocent purpose. I don't think, you know, he talks or acts like a murderer, this Scarborough. The young don't always mean just exactly what they say. Besides,' he added, and his smile reappeared again for a moment, 'I have promised to help you, and if I am to do that you must answer some questions.'

We settled down in a couple of arm-chairs, and I wondered whether this amateur detective would ask me the same questions as the professional had put to me before dinner.

'Forgive a foreigner's ignorance,' Brendel began, 'but do you wear gloves much in Oxford?'

'Why, no,' I replied. 'I suppose we don't. We wear them sometimes on very cold days to keep warm, and we wear them if we go up to London.'

'You wouldn't wear them to make a formal call – on the President or the Dean, for example?'

I laughed. 'Good Heavens, no; what an odd idea!'

Brendel nodded as though satisfied.

'Could you give me the names of the personal servants of everyone who dined last night? Scouts you call them, don't you? I learned that word yesterday.'

'Not off-hand,' I replied, 'but I will get a list for you to-morrow from the Bursar.'

'Could I look through their masters' wardrobes and cupboards with them?'

'It might seem a bit odd, but I suppose that if we said you were a detective it could be done. But they're a very trustworthy and loyal lot of men, and they won't much like it.'

Brendel nodded comprehendingly. 'It's not important, except in certain eventualities, and perhaps in a couple of cases.' He seemed to be talking to himself rather than to me, and for a minute or two he remained plunged in thought. Then he continued.

'There are four of your undergraduates that I must know more about. I have noted their names – yes – Scarborough, Garnett, Howe, Martin. Tell me something of them. Where they live, and what their fathers do, and any personal details you can think of.'

He noted the surprise in my face and laughed.

'There's no mystery, Winn. But I must talk with these young men, and the young are shy. If I know about them I can talk without scaring them, and there are perhaps things which they can tell me.'

I gave him the information he wanted, and was rewarded by some congratulatory remarks, which I admit gave me satisfaction.

'Excellent, excellent,' he said; 'really, you draw characters to perfection. You ought to write books, Winn, and give your gifts scope. Now tell me about all our friends who dined at the *Henkersmahlzeit*.'

Flattered by his praise I exerted myself to give a portrait of each of my colleagues in turn, whilst Brendel industriously made entries in his note-book.

'Just two more questions,' he said, when I had finished. 'First, do you own a car?'

'Yes,' I said, somewhat mystified. 'I don't use it much, but I've an old Standard in the garage behind the college.'

'May I borrow it when I need it?'

'Most certainly. I'll give you the garage key, and you can take it out when you wish.'

'Thank you, and now the last question. How can I meet and talk to Mrs Shirley and her sister?'

I hesitated and then answered him.

81

'With them we mustn't use any subterfuge. I couldn't be a party to that. The only way is to tell them straightforwardly that you are investigating this affair, and ask for their help. It will be painful, but I'll take you when you want to go.'

He thanked me, and shut up his note-book. I was surprised that he had asked me none of the questions about access to college and about the porters which had exercised Cotter's mind so much, and I mentioned my surprise to him.

He smiled. 'Your Inspector Cotter is highly competent,' he answered. 'He won't make any mistakes about that kind of thing. I've had already one little talk with him. He will do all that better than I could. And perhaps my method of approach is a little different from his. Good night.'

*

I saw little of him throughout Friday, though I knew from many stray remarks of others, and from my own observations, that he was busy throughout the day. I caught a glimpse of him driving in my car in the direction of Mottram's laboratory, I heard by chance from a friend in Balliol that he had called upon Tweddle, I heard that he had smoked and chatted in the rooms of Prendergast and Mitton and others, and that he had flattered Callendar by a request that the latter would show him our college silver and the Common Room cellar. For myself I was in a fever of disquiet over the thought of the inquest which was to take place on Saturday morning. I paced up and down my rooms, considering time after time how I should give my evidence. In vain I told myself that my own part in the proceedings was of very minor importance. My old nightmare thought that I should make a fool of myself, and appear ridiculous in public, gripped me once more. In imagination I saw myself stuttering or tongue-tied as the coroner posed his questions; I saw the expressions on the pale beautiful faces

82

of Ruth and Mary change from pity to surprise, even to contempt. I read too in advance the lurid accounts in the paper. Up to now the press had been admirably reticent. 'Well-known don shot in mysterious circumstances at Oxford. Investigations proceeding' had been a summary of all that had appeared. But after the inquest it would, I knew, be impossible to prevent a spate of hateful detail. I seemed to see a front-page picture of myself. 'F. W. Winn, Senior Tutor of St Thomas's, one of the first to see the murdered body', and above a miserable effigy of myself, old, feeble, and ineffective. In vain my reason told me that since I was neither corpse, nor murderer, nor even the first to discover the crime, I could not be starred as a protagonist by even the most unprincipled of journalists in search of copy. Instinct is stronger than reason, and no efforts could make me thrust myself into the decent obscurity of unimportance. My wretched habit of introspection and self-analysis tortured me. Again and again I went over in my mind my actions on that fatal evening. Should I not have prevented that ill-omened discussion on murder? Might I not, by a swift decision, have collected a band of eager helpers as soon as I saw Shirley's body, and with them have searched for and discovered the murderer before he could have escaped? Why had I not summoned the doctor before the police, and why had it taken me so long to fetch him? Half an hour earlier an experienced medical man might have been able to fix the time of the crime almost to a minute, and thus enabled us to trace the murderer. From nervous panic my mood changed to one of irritation. Why should the even tenor of my life be disturbed like this? For years I had lived the easy life of leisure and learning, hurting no one, content with my well-ordered, cultured, intellectual life. How easy it had always been over the port and coffee to discuss with enlightened and broad-minded calm the affairs of a troubled but

83

distant world! How liberal had been my views, how even and well-informed my judgement! And on the whole how well I had done it! That surely had been my *métier*.

> *Like Cato, give his little senate laws,*
> *And sit attentive to his own applause.*

That was how I had seen myself in the midst of my circle. Yes, Pope's words were curiously applicable, except that perhaps the applause had come from myself more than from my colleagues. And suddenly ugly facts had obtruded themselves and broken up my sheltered world. In a moment of insight I saw myself as perhaps I was; a weak, ineffective man too long protected from contact with realities, and now girding helplessly and bitterly against fate. And how would all this end? Could I hope to settle down again into the old groove? Should I float again serenely on the old sea of self-satisfaction? For the first time for more than thirty years I began to contemplate the thought of leaving Oxford, for a time at least. Many of my colleagues had taken to travel, to visit America or Australia or to go round the world, and I had mildly scoffed at their restlessness. 'Why,' I had once asked a returned and too voluble voyager with that gentle irony which I so much admired in myself, 'should events uninteresting in themselves acquire a profound importance because they occur in Singapore?' I remember how delicate the implied reproof had seemed to me. Yet might flight not now be my only salvation? Up and down I paced, arguing with myself, growing more irritated, more fretful, more unsettled with every hour that passed.

I had worked myself into a miserable state of indecision and panic by the time, just before dinner, when next I saw Brendel. I had almost decided, I think (if the word decided can be used of one so infirm of will), to leave Oxford at the earliest opportunity rather than to continue living in a society which included, as it seemed, an undiscovered

84

murderer. But five minutes of Brendel's society was enough to soothe my frayed nerves. He had an almost feminine intuition, and I believe that he read my thoughts and misgivings as though they had been written in an open book. He was all sympathy and encouragement. Exactly what he said I cannot now remember, only that his words were precisely suited to restore my lost confidence. There was something about the good fortune of the Common Room in having me to preside over it; something to the effect that any court or any jury would feel that because I had been there everything must of course have been ordered in the best possible way; a suggestion that I had handled the situation to admiration; a hint that I was now as before clearly the keystone of St Thomas's. It was just the tonic that I needed. Flattery no doubt it was, but it made me less abject than I had been before his visit. I felt myself again the Senior Tutor – if not quite *sans peur et sans reproche,* at least tolerably confident of my own adequacy.

# CHAPTER NINE

THE inquest was held on Saturday morning in one of the lecture rooms, and I wondered whether I should ever be able to bring myself to use that room again. To describe the scene in any detail would be superfluous, though every detail and every face is fixed deep in my memory. I have only to shut my eyes to see the scene again – the coroner, careful, courteous, decisive; Ruth and Mary both pale but bravely hiding their emotion; Hargreaves uneasy and embarrassed; Mottram obviously wretchedly ill, but, to judge from his looks, oblivious of his own trouble in his anxious sympathy for the President's daughters; Prendergast alert and watchful; Doyne healthy and strong, but temporarily subdued and downcast. The proceedings seemed to me both ghastly and interminable. I had to live again through the horror of that Wednesday evening. It was as though I was undergoing a frightful nightmare, from which I had suffered before. I knew from the beginning the horror would grow until it became overwhelming, yet nothing I could do would avert or hasten it. Point by point, piece by piece, the witnesses reconstructed the story. Everything seemed to me sordid, business-like, inexorable. I longed to cry out, 'Get on, get on; we know all this, for Heaven's sake finish with it.' At one moment I had an insane desire to shout out 'I killed him myself, don't ask any more questions' – if only I could thereby put a stop to the whole hateful inquiry. One by one we gave our evidence; clearly and more clearly the facts took shape in the minds of coroner and jury and reporters. Only for a short period did I experience a sort of unworthy satisfaction. Maurice Hargreaves was giving his evidence, and he was not cutting his usual fine figure. As a rule the most confident and self-assured of men, he was finding it exceedingly difficult to explain why he had left the revolver loaded on the table. The easy assurance that it would serve to impress the undergraduates in the morning with which he had countered my objections did not satisfy the coroner at all. He commented strongly, and with marked disapproval, on the Dean's behaviour. Maurice flushed and fumed, but for once he was muzzled. The provenance of the revolver was not disputed. Garnett admitted in the most barefaced manner that it was his, that he had always possessed one, and that he knew nothing about licences and such-like formalities. Scarborough was not called. As the inquest proceeded one thing became clear. No new fact or indication of any kind had come to light since I had last talked with Inspector Cotter. There was still no hint of any motive, still no clue, still no official theory of why the crime had been committed, or as to who the criminal might be.

The verdict was inevitable. Robbed of its official verbiage it amounted to this – that Shirley had been murdered, and that nobody knew by whom.

'What did you think of all that?' I asked Brendel as we crossed to my rooms after the verdict had been given. His answer was non-committal, and his smile enigmatic as he added:

'I think that you allowed yourself a little of what we Germans call *Schadenfreude*, did you not, when Mr Hargreaves gave his evidence?'

I had the grace to feel ashamed of myself, for I could not deny the accusation.

As we parted at the foot of my staircase he surprised me by a sudden request.

'Can you come to my rooms after dinner?' he said. 'I want to make a little experiment in which you can help me. It will take an hour or so. Please don't say No.'

'Of course I'll come,' I answered. 'What are you going to do?'

He wrinkled up his eyes in the fashion I now knew so well.

'Ah, just a little experiment. Perhaps I have not quite time to tell you about it now. After dinner; we will make it then.'

*

I was consumed with curiosity as I mounted Brendel's staircase that night, and my mystification did not grow less when I had entered his room. We had allotted him a spare set of rooms in one of which stood a large old-fashioned dining-table. Somewhere or other he had contrived to find or borrow a second table of the same kind, and the two were placed side by side so that the whole centre of the room seemed to be filled with one immense table. On this, to my great surprise, was laid out a large plan of St Thomas's, constructed of paper and cardboard. Brendel stood laughing at my amazement.

'I hope you admire my plan of St Thomas's,' he said. 'I'm sorry that it has to be on the flat, but I could not build a proper model with all the staircases and rooms. However, I think this will serve the purpose. Look at these.'

He held up a box full of cardboard discs. On each of them was written a name; I caught sight, on the top of the heap, of the names of Mitton, Doyne, and myself.

'I'm afraid I don't quite understand,' I said.

'Listen,' said Brendel. 'I want to reconstruct Wednesday night, and you must help me. Two heads are better than one, and there are some facts of which I must be sure. I want to go all through that evening; I want the conversations again, so far as we can remember them. I want the little incidents just as they occurred, and I want you to write down for me a little time-table as we go along. Come, let us begin at the beginning.'

He took up a small pair of forceps, selected two discs marked 'Prendergast' and 'Brendel', and placed them in the square in his plan which represented the Common Room.

'Here are Prendergast and I by the fire in the Common Room; it is about ten minutes, I think, before dinner, and you come in.'

He selected a third disc, marked 'Winn', and placed it by the other two.

'Now try to remember as much as you can of our conversation.'

'Brendel,' I said, 'is this really necessary? Must I really go through all that again? Surely we had enough of that at the inquest? To me it seems – well – ghoulish. I'll do it if you say I must, but can it possibly do any good?'

'I'm sorry,' he answered, 'but I'm afraid it is necessary. Look; if you call in a doctor you always take his advice – or discharge him, and for this case you have called in Dr Brendel. This is part of his prescription, and you must accept it, if you mean to benefit from his advice.'

He spoke lightly, but I could see that he was very anxious that I should not refuse, so I stifled my repugnance and promised my assistance.

'First rate,' he cried out with obvious relief; 'now then, it is half past seven, is it not, when we all go up to your beautiful Hall. Write that down, "Seven-thirty, dinner begins".'

As I wrote he sorted out thirteen discs, and placed them in position in the Hall on his plan. On each was written the name of one of the diners. With some little difficulty, after searching my recollection, I was able to place them in the order in which they had sat that night. He then took up three more, one marked 'Callendar' and the other two 'Servant', and placed them behind the diners.

'Now,' he said, 'we shall need all our memory. Between us we have to remember a conversation, or as much of it as possible, which took place three days ago.'

The task did not prove quite so impossibly difficult as I had anticipated. By jogging each other's memory we were able to recall the main threads of our conversation with tolerable accuracy. Gradually we traced it to the moment when Maurice had informed the table of the loaded revolver in his room.

'About when would that have been?' said Brendel.

'About eight, I should think; it was towards the end of dinner, because you and I had very little conversation about it.'

He nodded. 'Write down "Eight o'clock. Hargreaves tells us of the revolver", please, and tell me when we went down to the Common Room.'

'At about ten minutes past eight. It is always within five minutes of that when we get into Common Room.'

The thirteen discs were lifted and placed in Common Room; then he hesitated.

'Was Callendar in the room?'

'He came in with the port, and put it on the table; after that he came back once with a fresh bottle, and again, of course, with the coffee.'

'That creates a difficulty,' said Brendel thoughtfully. 'We can't possibly be quite sure what part of the conversation he heard, and what part he did not. On the whole it will be best to be on the safe side, and assume that he heard the whole conversation. Yes, that will be safe, surely. Now let's go on. We began to talk crime and detection as soon as we sat down?'

'Yes, I'm sure of that. Doyne started the ball rolling at once.' Carefully, assisting one another as best we could, we reconstructed the conversation. It was a curious sensation to hear Brendel repeating again the views which he had advanced in that long discussion. For myself I seemed to be living Wednesday evening over once again.

'When did coffee come in?' said Brendel at length.

'I can tell you that exactly,' I replied. 'Callendar has orders to bring it at twenty minutes to nine if I don't ring before, and on Wednesday I didn't ring. So it was at twenty minutes to nine.'

He nodded approvingly. 'Write it down. And then someone went out, I think?'

'Yes, Shepardson. He had a pupil at a quarter to nine, so he left then, and Mottram went at the same time to his lab.'

The forceps were lifted delicately and the discs of Mottram and Shepardson removed. The former was returned to the box, the latter placed in his own rooms in the plan. Two more discs were placed by him, marked 'Howe' and 'Martin'.

'And the next to move?'

My lips were dry as I answered.

'It was Shirley; he got up when the clock struck nine.'

Fascinated, I watched him pick up the disc which had 'Shirley' written on it, and place it carefully in the space which stood for Maurice Hargreaves' rooms.

'Callendar was in the room, clearing away,' he said meditatively. 'He told us that himself. He finished about nine-fifteen, and went out to find Scarborough and Garnett waiting for him.'

Two new discs appeared upon the table and were placed beside that of Callendar. I was conscious of a growing feeling of excitement and of fear. Almost it seemed to me as though one of the little discs would move on its own towards the fatal square where Shirley's disc lay. But Brendel went on calmly enough.

'And we were still talking about crime and criminals. Let me see, it's going to get more difficult now to remember who went out and when.'

But it was not very difficult after all. I was able to fix Doyne's exit at a quarter to ten, and with his that of the three scientists – Dixon, Tweddle, and Whitaker. Prendergast's appointment at ten made it equally easy to know

91

when his disc had to be lifted and conveyed to his room. Trower and Mitton had gone at the same time. In each case a disc was lifted and placed on another part of the table. Brendel, I noticed, knew without asking me where each of them had his rooms. He must have studied the movements of us all with scrupulous care since he had undertaken his task of investigation.

The drama of the situation gripped me more and more as I saw that only three discs were left in the space marked 'Common Room' – those of Brendel, Hargreaves, and myself. I had noted each time which we had 'agreed' carefully in my time-table; I now made another entry. '10.10, Hargreaves leaves Common Room.'

'How long was it before he came back?' said Brendel.

'Quite ten minutes, perhaps a little more, certainly not less.'

His estimate agreed with mine. Maurice, then, if his story was correct, must have remained about ten minutes in the Quad before he walked up to his rooms. I made another entry and Brendel thoughtfully picked up the discs bearing his name and my own, and placed them with those of Maurice and Shirley.

A frightful, and agonizing, curiosity possessed me. Which of all those discs lying on different parts of the table was acting a passive lie? Which of them, if any, ought to have been lifted and placed beside the disc of Shirley at the moment when the shot had been fired? Or should there not have been some other disc, one yet unnamed, which should have been placed there, the disc perhaps, as Mitton had thought, of some desperate homicidal maniac, who was still unsuspected in our midst?

Brendel was looking at the table with a curious expression, as though he had resolved some doubts and arrived at a result which he both expected and disliked.

'I don't think we need go on any longer,' he said. 'But

can you think of anything important which we have omitted?'

I thought carefully for a few minutes.

'What about Callendar's boy?' I said at length. 'He came into the Common Room with Callendar to clear away, and must have heard Shirley saying that he would go up and wait for Hargreaves. He's not very bright, but still he probably noticed what was being said.'

Brendel emitted a long-drawn-out whistle.

'Thank you, Winn. Which goes to show that one may miss important things however careful one tried to be. Was this boy up in Hall as well at dinner-time? I mean, could he have heard also what Hargreaves said about the revolver? And what sort of age is he? I took no proper notice of him.'

'He's about seventeen. Yes. He probably was up in Hall, but he'd be on the move up there, waiting and so on, and very probably didn't hear about the revolver.'

'Well, I must have a talk with him in the morning,' said Brendel. 'There's a possible leakage there; a possible flaw in Prendergast's theory – and I missed it. I'm very grateful to you for keeping me straight there, very grateful indeed.'

He began methodically to collect his discs and put them back into the box. As he did so I glanced at the clock, and was amazed to see that our 'reconstruction' of the evening of Wednesday had taken us a couple of hours; I had been so enthralled that the time had passed as though it had been a short half-hour.

Brendel laughed when I drew his attention to the time.

'Yes,' he said, 'it took a long time, but I think it may have been very useful. By the way, is the funeral to be on Monday?'

'Yes. The first part of the service is to be in the College Chapel, and the rest at the cemetery by the station. I suppose that only the relatives and poor Shirley's colleagues will go down to the cemetery. Somehow we shall have to prevent a crowd of people who only want to gape out of morbid curiosity.'

'You won't exclude me, I hope; I want to be there particularly.'

'Of course not; naturally you can come if you wish.'

He had finished his tidying up by now, and I was preparing to say good night, but he made one more request.

'You said that you would arrange for me to see Mrs Shirley and Miss Vereker. I hate to have to question them, but if it can be arranged, I must. May I see them to-morrow?'

'Yes. I'll ask them if they will see you to-morrow evening. Would some time about five or six suit you?'

'Perfectly, and I shall be much obliged to you. And if you in your turn will keep an hour free after dinner for me I think that I shall have some interesting things to tell you – unless, of course, Inspector Cotter has arrested the criminal already before then. But somehow I don't think he will have.'

We made our arrangements accordingly, and wished each other good night.

# CHAPTER TEN

SUNDAY in Oxford had always been a pleasant day for me. I was not one of those who had fallen a victim to golf, or who used my week-end to hurry away into the country. My habit always was to refresh myself by making Sunday a real day of relaxation. And so I would get up at a later hour, shave more slowly than usual, and dawdle over my breakfast. Then after the service in the College Chapel I would idle away the rest of the morning, entertain two or three friends to lunch and then go for a stroll round the Parks or for a short drive in the car. I not infrequently took a cup of tea with the Verekers and then read or dozed in my rooms until it was time for dinner and Common Room and the conversation which I loved. A day of leisure and ease and contentment. But with the shadow of an unexplained crime hanging over the college it was impossible to hope for the customary calm. Nor indeed had I quite finished my breakfast when Inspector Cotter was announced with the request that I would favour him with a quarter of an hour of my time. I sighed rather wearily and told my servant to bring him in.

He started without preamble, and my heart sank at his first words.

'I want you, sir, if you will, to tell me all that you can about a Mr Scarborough, who is an undergraduate here. He was, I understand, a friend of the owner of the revolver, and I discovered last night that he knew that Mr Shirley was in the Dean's rooms, and that he made some very ugly remarks about him too. Yes, some very ugly remarks – something about shooting him if he had the chance.'

'How did you know that?' I asked involuntarily. Surely Callendar could not have spoken about his interview with Scarborough except to me; yet the Inspector had apparently wormed out the whole history of that unfortunate meeting.

He gave me a keen and almost suspicious glance. 'I heard, sir, from Callendar's boy. He came out of the Common Room pantry at the same time as Callendar and seems to have – er – contrived to hear most of a highly interesting conversation.'

Inwardly I consigned Callendar's boy to the lowest place in Hades. I had thought him dull and stupid, and had told Brendel that he was unlikely to have listened intelligently to any conversation. Now it appeared that he had missed very little indeed.

'There's another thing sir. I think that Callendar told you all about that conversation up here on Thursday night.'

His tone now was definitely challenging and hostile. I felt like a lad caught out in the act of committing some misdemeanour.

'Yes,' I answered, putting the best face I could on the situation. 'He did tell me, but I thought it unnecessary to tell anyone else of a few wild remarks of that kind. But however did you know that Callendar had told me?'

'The boy told me. He noticed that Callendar was very worried, and when he watched him come up to your rooms he put two and two together and guessed that you were being put wise about Mr Scarborough. That boy'll get on in life, sir.'

Inwardly I cursed the boy with redoubled vehemence. He was clearly much too sharp and much too interested in other people's business. And I had dismissed him from my mind as a dullard. For the time being, however, I had enough to do to placate Cotter.

'I'm sorry I didn't tell you,' I said. 'It was wrong of me, of course, but I know this young Scarborough pretty well, and it didn't seem right to draw him into all this more than was necessary.'

'Precisely,' said Cotter in a voice so dry as to be almost offensive. 'You know him very well ... Really, sir, I'm bound to say that I think it was foolish of you not to take me into your confidence. It's delayed things a good deal. I suppose there's nothing else that you would wish to tell me that you've kept to yourself? If I'm to bring this thing off I must get all the help I can.'

'No, indeed,' I said warmly. 'There's nothing else; I assure you that I've concealed absolutely nothing from you.'

The Inspector seemed to accept my assurance, and appeared somewhat mollified.

'Very well,' he said. 'Then perhaps you'd kindly tell me all you can about Scarborough. I haven't seen him yet, but I shall examine him and his movements pretty closely to-day, and I want to know all I can about him before I start.'

*

When Cotter left I was the prey to the most gloomy forebodings. The more I considered the case the more did it appear very ugly for Scarborough. Brendel, it is true, had assured me that he did not suspect him, but I could not help reflecting that Brendel was both a foreigner and an amateur. Cotter, on the other hand, was an experienced professional, whose methods might be slower and less subtle, but who might be expected to arrive at the truth by the orthodox means. If he really supposed that Scarborough was guilty, was it not at least possible that he was right? What ought I to do? I dared not warn Scarborough of the ordeal before him, even had I thought it wise to do so. I could hardly in the circumstances appeal to Brendel for advice. If I sought help from any other of my colleagues I should only raise suspicions of Scarborough in their minds. Finally I decided that I must write to his father. If indeed his son was in danger of being arrested for murder it could not be wrong to warn Fred Scarborough of the peril in which he stood. I sat down and narrated the whole story as clearly and succinctly as I could. Even so it was a long letter by the

time I had finished it, and I dropped it into the letter-box
with a sigh of relief.

*

Just before six Brendel came to fetch me, for Ruth and
Mary had agreed to see him in the President's Lodgings that
evening, and I was to go over with him. They were sitting in
a room which I knew well, a small drawing-room next to the
President's study. Both of them, I thought, looked tired and
ill in their black clothes, but nothing could make them seem
other than beautiful to me. I forgot my own selfish anxieties
and annoyance as I thought of the suffering which they must
have undergone in the last few days. Brendel was full of
solicitude, and, as it seemed to me, his apologies for the intrusion were almost overdone. In some way he appeared to
me more foreign than he usually did. Often I had had to
remind myself that he was not an Englishman, but now a
sort of foreign ornateness of speech and manner was very
noticeable to me. His excuses and his thanks to the ladies
for receiving him were courteous but over-elaborate. I found
myself wondering whether he was temperamentally unable
to put himself *en rapport* with women in the same way as he
could with men, or whether perhaps he was disguising a
failure to make headway in his inquiry by a camouflage of
energy and officiousness. My faint dissatisfaction grew as
the interview proceeded, for Brendel's questions when they
came were disappointingly trivial and unilluminating. He
made exactly those banal inquiries which I should have
expected from an ordinary detective. When had Shirley left
home? Had he seemed in any way anxious or nervous before
he left the house in North Oxford? Had he ever received any
threatening letters? Did Mrs Shirley know of any private
enemies of her husband's? I had come, in the last few days,
to like and trust Brendel so much that I was keenly disappointed as the interview proceeded. I suppose that I
expected some penetrating questions from him which would

suddenly throw new light on the problem. Moreover, as I watched and listened, I was conscious of a curious fact. Brendel was addressing himself to Ruth, but his whole attention was really devoted to Mary. Of this fact I became more and more certain, and it filled me with disquiet.

After perhaps ten minutes or a quarter of an hour Brendel thanked Ruth for her patience, and inquired if he might ask Miss Vereker a few questions also. Mary, of course, agreed, though I could see that she was surprised at the request. I was now again on the tiptoe of expectation, but again I was disappointed. The questions which were put to Mary were more pointless, as it seemed to me, even than those which Ruth had answered. I felt convinced that Brendel was talking merely for the sake of talking, and that no useful information was being elicited. At length he said, with the air of a man who has almost reached the end of a task which he has set himself:

'One more thing, Miss Vereker; I want if I may to ask rather a personal question. You are engaged to be married, are you not?'

Mary Vereker shared her father's fastidious dislike of publicity, and I could see that she considered the question ill-timed if not impertinent. What possible connexion could her own private affairs have with the tragedy of her brother-in-law's death? For a moment I thought that she was going to administer a snub to her interrogator, but she restrained herself, and replied frigidly in the affirmative.

'And have you in the last few days – forgive me for the question – had any little misunderstandings, any small quarrels with your fiancé?'

Mary was really angry now, and she showed it. For a bachelor there are few sights more stimulating than a beautiful woman in a temper, but I admit that I was glad that I was not in Brendel's shoes just then.

'Professor Brendel,' she said, 'I do not know why you

ask me such a question. My affairs have, I think, nothing whatever to do with the tragedy which you are investigating. I promised Mr Winn that I would answer your questions, and so I will tell you that I have had no kind of quarrel with Maurice, nor any sort of misunderstanding. But I cannot undertake to discuss my private affairs any further with a stranger, and I do not believe that Mr Winn would wish me to do so.'

'No, indeed,' I hastily interjected, for I had been appalled at Brendel's remark. 'I am sure that no good purpose could be served by any more discussion. I feel certain that Professor Brendel will not wish to trouble you any more.'

Brendel was profuse in his apologies. In pursuing his inquiries he had not sufficiently considered that such questions must give pain to Miss Vereker; he was desolated at his own clumsiness; he hoped that he might be excused for his quite unintentional rudeness. Very stiffly Mary accepted his apology, and he bade the two ladies adieu.

I did not go with him, but stayed behind to smooth down the troubled waters. It was no very easy task. The purport of Brendel's questions had not been clear to any of us, but their general trend was obvious enough. If his questions had any significance whatever he had surely been suggesting the possibility of sordid quarrels and misunderstandings in Shirley's family circle. The questions which he had put to Mary seemed to me, as they had to her, purely impertinent. I tried to explain them away as the clumsy *faux pas* of an amateur investigator, who was searching blindly for some chance clue; but I could see that in the minds of both ladies the reputation of Brendel was hopelessly ruined.

\*

Brendel was dining at All Souls that evening, and had told me that he would come to my rooms at about ten o'clock. I

100

waited for him in a state of considerable exasperation, and prepared rather carefully what would be, I felt, at once a tactful yet severe reproof. I ·was pondering in my mind whether it would be wise to suggest to him that it might be safer, after all, to leave the investigation in official hands, when he knocked and came in. But I had no opportunity to broach the subject, for before I could open my mouth he had patted me twice on the back as though I were a child needing comfort, and was launched on a flood of words which I could not easily stem.

'You were going to say, if I had let you, my dear friend, that the poor blundering Austrian Professor had made an intolerable *gaffe*; that he had been terribly rude to your quite charming ladies in the President's Lodgings; that he did not quite understand the conventions of English society; that in short he had made a real mess of all your business; that perhaps even, yes, perhaps he ought to give up the work of detection and leave it to those who understand it better. Now, admit, you were going to say all that, very tactfully yet very firmly; were you not?'

Somehow as he spoke all my old confidence and belief in him returned to me, but I could not help admitting that his prognosis was almost literally true.

'Yes,' I said a little sheepishly. 'I suppose I was going to say something of the kind. You know really in those questions to Mary Vereker you went too far; both she and her sister were terribly upset. And I was upset too. I've known them both so long and I like them so much. I really consider myself – well – more or less I'm in a sort of semi-paternal relation to them, poor girls. I feel for them more than I can say, and naturally they resented your questions, just as I did.'

I was working myself into a state of indignation again, but Brendel soothed me with a reassuring gesture of the hand.

'My dear Winn,' he said, 'indeed, as you say, they are

the most charming young ladies, I find it in my heart to envy you – what is it? – your semi-paternal status in that household. Consider now. Do you really think that I can have liked asking them those very awkward and unpleasant questions? Am I quite such a heartless Philistine, am I really so little of what you call a gentleman to enjoy a task like that? I tell you I was quite nervous, quite uncomfortable all the time. I felt like one of your youngest undergraduates facing you for the first time, and finding you in a bad temper.' All the little crow's-feet round his eyes puckered up as he smiled at me. I knew that he was laughing at me and at my annoyance, but it was impossible for me to take offence or to maintain my censorious attitude towards him. I surrendered once more to his odd charm and power.

'No, no,' he went on, 'I hated having to do it. It hurt me to ask those questions. But they were quite, quite necessary. You must believe that, and trust me a little if I am to help you. I can't tell you now just why I had to ask them, but I will tell you this. I like and admire your Miss Vereker, almost as much as she disapproves of me, and I'm very glad that she answered just as she did. But what a snub I got! Well, I must get over that. And now do remember that I only started on this investigation because you begged me to – so please let us have the old confidence, or we shan't make progress.'

I could hardly have resisted his appeal even if I had wished to do so, and I decided at once to tell him the whole ugly history of Cotter's visit that morning, and of the latter's suspicions of Scarborough. I had settled in my mind before Brendel arrived that I should say nothing of all this to him, but now I felt strongly the need for his advice and support. So I poured out the whole wretched story of Cotter's discovery of Scarborough's connexion with the revolver, and of the suspicions which, in the Inspector's mind and my own, were making the case grow blacker and blacker with regard to that unfortunate young man. Finally I told him how I had written to Scarborough's father, so that he might be warned of the danger in which his son stood.

To my intense astonishment he broke into a roar of laughter. 'Forgive me,' he said. 'I ought not to laugh, but it is really very funny. The Inspector had not seen Scarborough when he talked to you?'

'No, he had not. But by now he may have put the wretched boy on the rack and, for all I know, have dragged a confession out of him. It's too awful, and I'm more or less responsible for him up here.'

Brendel patted me again on the shoulder.

'No, no, don't worry,' he said. 'I assure you on my word of honour that your young protégé is as safe from suspicion as you are, or as I am. And by now the good Inspector certainly knows that too. He was just what you would call one lap behind. When you've heard what I have to tell you, you'll know all about that. Settle yourself down comfortably in your chair, and get ready for a long story. I want to tell you all about my luncheon party and a lot of other things as well.'

# CHAPTER ELEVEN

WE sat down on each side of the fire; I lit a pipe and composed myself to listen.

'To-day,' he began, 'I had my little luncheon party. Two days ago I invited them, and they all accepted. There came – let me see –' He held up four rather chubby fingers and ticked off his guests on them. 'First your Scarborough, then his friend Garnett, and the young man Martin and his friend Howe. From your quite excellent descriptions of them on Thursday night I knew already a great deal of each of them. And so everything is as natural, as natural as can be. Look!' He held up his four fingers again. 'Of Scarborough's father I heard so much from you that I am a friend of his early days. Garnett has lived for two years in Mexico, and I have studied Mexico in your college library with all the encyclopaedias for nearly two days, and he will never guess that I have not really had those six months there that I described so picturesquely! Of course I must ask my fellow-Mexican to lunch! And then Howe and Martin; that is really most curious! My friend Martyn with whom years ago I used to shoot in Norfolk spells his name with a Y, and so I am quite wrong in thinking that the Martin here is a relation of his! And my old business correspondent How, in the City of London, has no E in his name, and my guest of to-day has! What an extraordinary coincidence, so extraordinary that it must be true! If you invent something sufficiently absurd in all its details people will always believe it. How we all five laughed at the thought of a luncheon party where two of the guests had been asked because the host thought that their names had been spelt differently! Four guests and two of them there under false pretences! And so there we were all as happy as possible; no stiffness, no discussion of your quite execrable Oxford climate, no polite inquiries about the state of the University at Vienna. No *Zwang,* as we say, at all. Of course they called me "Sir" a little too often at first, and were just a little too polite, but that soon passed, for I had taken my precautions.'

He paused to relight his cigar, and to smile at me.

'There were no cocktails, because they would have been unsuited to your great traditions, but the estimable Callendar had provided me with some very admirable sherry, an Amontillado of great merit. The young, as I have often observed, are fond of discussing wine, so I ask them at once for their opinion. I think it really good, but is it perhaps the slightest degree too dry? Scarborough rolls it round his tongue, and says that for his taste sherry should be dry, and that it is excellent. And Howe commends it, and Martin praises it, and Garnett, who is a little older – isn't he – than the others, continues to say nothing, but he drinks two glasses whilst the others are criticizing one. So we are already all good friends when we start lunch, and over that lunch I have taken very great trouble. It is a good lunch, Winn; let me say your cook is a great ornament and credit to your college. With our lunch we drink a Clos de Vougeot of 1911, specially commended to me by Callendar. And again I invite the criticism of these connoisseurs. Though I speak as host it really does seem to me a worthy wine, but do they think it if anything just a little lacking in body? Scarborough, who has been very well brought up, thinks it an admirable wine, but agrees that if any criticism could be offered it would be just precisely that one which I have suggested. Howe is full of encomiums, and Martin hazards some praise of the bouquet. Garnett offers no special contribution to the discussion, but the greater part of the bottle finds its way into his glass. I suggest that perhaps the second bottle will by chance be better than the first, since bottles differ so much. And my little party begins to go very well.

'Sooner or later, of course, we must talk of the murder, though it is not I who first mention it. What do I think of it, they ask? I shrug my shoulders, and explain that I am of course a stranger here, and I can know nothing of the people concerned, or how this dreadful thing can have happened. But what do *they* think of it? And who was really the murderer, and how did he get away unobserved? Then they all begin to talk at once – (except Garnett who is filling his glass) – and I – well – I listen. But for you, my dear Winn, I shall disentangle their most interesting stories.'

Brendel fancies himself not a little as a raconteur, and he now made a dramatic pause, and smacked his hand on the arm of his chair. 'Ah,' he said, 'I've forgotten the most important thing of all! Now listen!'

'Nonsense,' I said, 'you haven't forgotten anything. I'm not taken in so easily. You're just working up the effects.'

He laughed. 'Well, perhaps. But you must forgive the tricks of the old lecturer. I'm just underlining the important things for you, so be patient, and don't spoil my little story.'

'Go on,' I said. 'I'm too old to be kept in suspense like this. You're like an old lady at the card-table who won't play out her trumps.'

'Not at all. I am that rare creature, a lawyer with a true sense of the dramatic. Besides, it's better than a trump, or even than the ace of trumps. It is the joker which I shall now play, and the joker will make all your poor Inspector Cotter's little trumps look quite shabby. Are you ready?'

'Yes, for heaven's sake, let's have it out,' I replied, half amused and half exasperated.

'Well, it's only this. I quite forgot to say – now don't contradict me – I *quite* forgot to say that your friend Scarborough came to my little party with the fingers of his right hand all bandaged up . . .'

'But . . .'

'There are no buts about it. Listen to me. The young man shows me his hand, and curses his ill-fortune. (How little, my dear Winn, we understand our own best interests!) He tells me how he spoke to Callendar (we knew that!) and how he and Garnett went on to join the party which was celebrating your rowing victories. And since he was just a little – oh, just a very little – intoxicated, and since fireworks are dangerous things, he contrived to blow off a nice little bit of the first and second fingers of his right hand. What happens next? Of course his friend Garnett is there to help him, and by happy chance the Head Porter is there too; between them they bandage up the damaged hand; they go into Garnett's rooms and smear a lot of grease over the wounds and tear up a handkerchief or two, and the thing's done. Yes, I've seen Mr Pine and it's all correct. Five or ten minutes after he spoke those very incriminating words to Callendar, Scarborough was being bandaged up by Pine and Garnett. I daresay they didn't bandage him very skilfully, but they did it quite well enough. Have you ever tried, Winn, to shoot a man with a revolver when your right hand has just been roughly bandaged by the Head Porter? Of course you haven't, and, if you ever do, you'll miss. Scarborough's got a grand alibi, and nothing can shake it. Providence, as you must have observed in the course of your career, has a wonderful way of watching over the young and the intoxicated. He might have blown out one of his eyes and have been blind for life, he might have remained unhurt at all, and then he would have been considered by suspicious persons like you and Cotter as a murderer. But, no! He damages his hand just enough to give himself a cast-iron alibi at the cost of three weeks' inconvenience. Really Providence is wonderful! And he, poor young man, is so blind to his good fortune, that all he can say is that it was damnable to be knocked out just then, because otherwise he and Garnett would probably have been cruising (yes, that was the word) round the Quad, and would no doubt have spotted the murderer on his way towards the crime. Incidentally Scarborough's alibi secures Garnett as well; the pair of them were together all the evening. I noticed that you didn't observe that one was as much implicated as the other, or that of the two Garnett was much the more likely to have committed a deed of violence. I'm afraid, Winn, that you let your personal feelings sway you too much for successful detective work! But Scarborough was lucky, all the same. And why did he want to see Shirley that night? Just because he had what he called a tutorial the next day, and he wanted to postpone it. Shirley was always difficult, but sometimes a little more approachable after a good dinner. How very, very simple!'

Brendel puffed a cloud of smoke triumphantly into the air and looked questioningly at me.

'You don't seem quite so pleased at my little joker card as I expected,' he said.

I had indeed been unable to conceal my embarrassment. 'Of course I'm delighted,' I said, 'but I'm frightfully put out about that letter to Fred Scarborough. You see, I put it all very strongly. I told him that his son was suspected of murder, that the facts looked very awkward for him, that he was really in a grave predicament, and that Fred ought to come up at once. What the devil am I to do now? I shall look a perfect fool, and Fred Scarborough will never speak to me again.'

The laugh with which Brendel greeted my plaint seemed to me rather unfeeling.

'Dear, dear,' he said, 'and now *you* are in a "very grave predicament." Well, you must wire as early as you can to-morrow morning and ask him to burn your letter unread. For me, I find the situation piquant. Your old friend will sit down to his hearty English breakfast. Naturally he will read first the telegram which lies on the top of his letters. Every human instinct will then impel him to open the fat envelope, addressed to him in your handwriting, which lies by his plate. The training which he has laboriously received at his expensive public school and at St Thomas's will urge him with equal force to obey your request. The struggle will be terrible. Will he succumb to the temptation or will he not? Really a most dramatic situation! I think you must word that telegram very strongly, and perhaps it would be wise to prepay the reply. Ask him to let you know that he *has* destroyed the letter unread. We ought to weigh the scale a little in favour of St Thomas's training if we can; human curiosity is dreadfully strong on the other side. Don't worry, Winn,' he went on more seriously, as he noted my real distress, 'honestly I don't think you need be nervous, and you must keep up a standard of relative values. After all, the solid fact is that the young man is as safe from suspicion as you or I. Furthermore, the laborious Cotter, my rival in detection, has by now discovered the fact, and is kicking himself for having wasted another half-day on a false scent. But don't write unnecessary letters again if you want to be a successful detective. And isn't it better sometimes' (his eyes twinkled as he spoke) 'to overcome your natural shyness and ask a few awkward or even discourteous questions even at the expense of a snub? If you could have brought yourself to have inquired of your young protégé if he was murdering anyone that night, he would just have waved his bandaged hand in your face, and you need never have written to his father. There's something in the straightforward question and answer method, you know. But surely no harm has really been done.'

With my confidence partly restored I composed myself to listen to the rest of Brendel's story.

'The tale of Howe and Martin was no less interesting,' he said. 'Let me see, how did you describe them to me on

Thursday night? "A pair of good, normal, rather simple young men, not really academically-minded." How true!'

From anyone else I should have felt disposed to resent the mimicry of myself, which I thought I could detect, but I was beyond the stage of resenting any of Brendel's little habits, so I made no comment, and he continued.

'Listen then to the true tale of the two not academically-minded young men, as drawn from them by my Clos de Vougeot.'

He chuckled, and settled himself deeper into his chair as he continued his story. If the mimicry of myself had been doubtful and in slightly bad taste, that of the under-graduates was obvious and wholly amusing. The speaker was Brendel, but it seemed to me at times as though I was really listening to the voices of his Sunday guests.

'"You see," Martin said, "we went up, Howe and I, to do our weekly tutorial with the Sheep – I beg your pardon, Sir, with Mr Shepardson. And it so happened that we hadn't done the work he'd set us." "By a curious coincidence," Howe interjected, "the same thing had happened the week before, too." "Precisely," said Martin, "and the Sheep, though a mild creature by nature and upbringing, had then shown unsuspected tigerish qualities. A fresh display of temper, unworthy of our tutor, was therefore, we felt, if possible, to be averted." "That," chorused Howe, "was exactly our intention." "We therefore considered whether an appeal to his higher nature, or a well-phrased request for a moratorium might not melt his stony heart, and decided that we knew a trick worth two of that." [I have,' interpolated Brendel, with obvious satisfaction, 'added considerably to my stock of English idioms as a result of my luncheon party. The more obscure phrases I noted down directly in my note-book, so I think they are correct, though I did not always fully understand them.] "Yes, we knew a trick worth two of that, so we put out a little bait." "And the Sheep swallowed it line and all," chimed in the faithful Howe.' [Brendel looked at me inquiringly. 'A piscatorial metaphor not usually applied to Sheep,' I explained.] '"Before he could ask for the proses which we had not done, I said, all innocent like, 'Please, Sir, I'd like to ask you a question before we get to work. Howe and I went to a lecture at New College to-day on Juvenal, and the lecturer seemed to think that two of Mr Shirley's suggested emendations in the text of the third Satire might possibly be mistaken. I've brought the text along to ask you.' 'Possibly be wrong,' snorts the Sheep, 'possibly be wrong ... obviously, palpably, manifestly, ridiculously wrong! Give me the text for a moment and let me show you. And remember always, both of you, that wild speculative guesses are *not* scholarship.' Right off the deep end he goes at once,"' [Brendel looked at me with a puzzled air, as he recounted this passage. 'Deep end of what? A sheep or something else?' 'A swimming bath, I think,' I said, 'but the phrase is obscure.'] '"Well, the Sheep didn't want much egging on after that. He got blood to the head in a way that was pretty to watch. He took a hold of the text and showed us one mistake of Shirley's after another. But the trouble was that once he'd smelt blood we couldn't stop him; hot on the scent and head down and all that. He showed us about one hundred instances which proved beyond all reasonable doubt that Shirley was a reckless and ill-informed person. Good, bitter scholarly back-chat it was too. At last we couldn't stand any more. We'd got up at a quarter to nine, ten o'clock had struck, and the Sheep was still hitting poor old Shirley for sixes all round the ground."' [Brendel shook his head helplessly as he disinterred this phrase from his notebook. 'A cricketing phrase,' I explained, 'and incomprehensible to anyone born outside England. Go on.'] '"It was pretty clear that we had to make an effort, so I kicked Howe under the table" ["unnecessarily hard," muttered the chorus] "and said, with the innocence of a new-born babe, that it seemed that Shirley was a pretty dangerous sort of chap for us to get into touch with. Didn't the Sheep think that we ought to give up going to his lectures in case our minds might be corrupted? Well, the Sheep began to see that he'd gone a bit too far in crabbing a colleague, so he stopped in his mad career, and said that we mustn't take everything he said *au pied de la lettre,* that perhaps he'd overstated things a trifle, that Shirley was, of course, a great scholar, though fundamentally wrong in all his views about Juvenal, and that we must certainly not abstain (my God, what a word!) from his lectures, and that, well, it was getting late, and that he was glad we were so keenly interested in textual criticism, and, that, in short, we might go, and might bring him a couple of proses each next week. We didn't exactly take long in making our dignified exit, and as we came out we saw the Dean in the Quad, standing just under the windows of his own rooms. And that's the damnable thing again! If we'd shut down the Sheep's blitherings half an hour earlier we might easily have seen the chap who went and shot up poor old Shirley."'

Brendel paused, and then added dryly, 'And that is the end of the saga of the two normal rather simple young men, who are not academically-minded. It was also the end of my little party. I forgot to say that I had provided a bottle of that very excellent Taylor '08 port, in case the burgundy failed to loosen tongues. It was about this time that my Mexican guest, who had listened without interruption to Martin's tale, got up and intimated courteously that it was time for him to be going. I observed that the port was finished. So they all thanked me, and we parted with the warmest expressions of mutual esteem.'

# CHAPTER TWELVE

BRENDEL'S face was a perfect network of wrinkles. 'That was the end of my party, and a very satisfactory end, too. Consider. Scarborough is cleared, I am sure, beyond all fear of suspicion. But more important than that, Shepardson is safe as well. You noticed that, surely. It was the chief object of all my manoeuvres to make sure about that. Now we know with absolute certainty that Martin and Howe were with him until Hargreaves came into the Quad. Could Shepardson possibly have visited Hargreaves' rooms and murdered Shirley in that short interval whilst Hargreaves was standing below in the Quad, or walking round it? I suggest that you've only got to put the question, and consider the difficulties, to arrive at your answer. Of course he couldn't have done it! Shepardson has his alibi, and I must confess that I'm relieved. I never really thought he was the criminal, but the actions and reactions of these learned and disputatious men are difficult to predict, and I couldn't disguise from myself that he *might* have done it. Now he's cleared. Yes, it was really a very satisfactory luncheon party for me. I've established the innocence of two of the suspects, I've learned a lot of new idioms, and of your famous Oxford educational methods I have now the most vivid picture.' He chuckled again at the recollection of Howe and Martin with their tutor. 'Young men don't differ much all over the world, in Vienna or Oxford or anywhere else. Murderers don't differ much either,' he added in a changed and rather grim voice. 'There is always plan and motive and opportunity, and our murderer is still amongst us.'

It seemed to me a long time before he spoke again. He appeared to be lost in a reverie, in which I did not feel disposed to disturb him, but at length he re-lit his cigar and continued his narrative.

'I've done some other things besides entertaining under-graduates to lunch, and you must hear about them. Scarborough is cleared and so is Shepardson, so we can dismiss them from our minds; but if I remember rightly Prendergast drew up a list of eight suspects – you probably remember that list?'

'I'm not likely to forget it, though the whole theory was hateful to me, and I don't believe in it. His eight suspects were himself, Shepardson, Mitton, Trower, Mottram, Hargreaves, Tweddle of Balliol and Doyne. I think that was the lot.'

'Yes, and we've cleared Shepardson, or rather his pupils have, so that leaves us seven. And I fancy that my researches have made some of them pretty safe too. If you'll listen I'll run through the list.'

He opened his note-book and studied it for a moment. 'First there's Trower. I've got no certain evidence to clear him, and yet I'm sure that he can be eliminated. He went out at ten o'clock with Mitton; he said that he started to go through some accounts, and then went to sleep in his chair. Highly suspicious of course, but one small fact makes me sure it's true. It's just this. In spite, my dear Winn, of the brilliance of our conversation after dinner your gallant Major certainly went to sleep for quite five minutes in Common Room soon after we had had coffee. As a stranger I was observing you all pretty closely, and I'm certain I wasn't deceived about that. Of course these military men are accustomed to take a rest when they can get it, but I simply can't believe that he would have had a nap half-an-hour before committing a brutal murder. And if by some extraordinary chance he had, why then he would have invented a better or at least a different explanation of his post-murder occupation than another forty winks. No. I just can't fit him into the chief part, and I've crossed him off the list. Then there's Mr Tweddle of Balliol. I've explored him a bit, and I confess that I laid a few traps for him.'

'What do you mean by that?' I asked.

Brendel smiled. 'Oh, the ordinary kind of trap. With the aid of the introductions you gave me I made my way into Balliol society and contrived to meet Tweddle in the Common Room there. I reminded him of our former meeting, professed to be interested in those ghastly subjects which he professes, and asked him round here to my rooms. He accepted. You'll find my room, I said, on the next staircase to Hargreaves'. His face was a complete blank; he didn't know who Hargreaves was, nor where his rooms were. I watched him pretty closely, and I'll swear he hadn't the remotest idea as to Hargreaves' domicile, and why should he, unless he was the murderer? But a man who has committed a crime is always expecting awkward questions of that kind, and guarding himself against the wrong answer. He's got to be what you call a pretty cool hand not to give himself away by admitting knowledge which he ought not to have, or by disguising it too obviously. Again, I mentioned Mrs Shirley quite casually in the course of conversation, and found that he had no idea that such a person existed. Of course he may have been deceiving me all the time; he may have coached himself to make just the right answer to every question, but I can't bring myself to believe that he is the sort of man to do that. Besides, I couldn't find any connexion whatever between him and anyone in St Thomas's except your scientists. The more I probed the more firmly I became convinced that his head has room for no other subject than higher mathematics. I therefore crossed him off the list also; he need never have been on it if he'd had the ordinary common sense to remember to take his scarf with him that evening. If he'd remembered it he'd have saved me a lot of trouble. However I'm quit of him now. As soon as I got back to college I telephoned to him to say that I had stupidly forgotten a previous engagement at the time at which I had invited him round here, and that I'd write later to suggest another date. But I never shall – the life of the detective imposes its duties, but a *tête-à-tête* with Mr Tweddle on higher mathematics is more than I can be expected to endure unless I must.'

He drew a line firmly through Tweddle's name in his notebook and turned to the next page.

'Then we come to Doyne and Mitton,' he remarked with an involuntary smile. 'Let's dispose of them. I suppose that a master in the art of detection would have turned them inside out by now. Their alibis were wretched or non-existent, and each of them had the opportunity to shoot Shirley. I'd better confess to you right away that I've paid no attention to them whatever, beyond taking a cup of tea one day with Mitton, and chatting with both of them in Common Room. I simply can't begin to suspect either of them. Mitton is the gentlest of men, who wouldn't hurt a fly; he'd blush too much to take aim with any lethal weapon; – and Doyne – well, he'd make so much noise about the job, and be so cheerful over the preliminaries that everyone would come along to see the crime. Seriously, how can one think of either of them as a criminal? Of course in books mild young men in Holy Orders and light-hearted care-free young fellows like Doyne are the very stuff out of which criminals of almost incredible turpitude can be constructed, but surely it's not so in real life. I can't and I won't keep either of them on my list, and if I'm wrong I'll never study another crime.'

There was another pause whilst Brendel crossed out the names of Mitton and Doyne, and turned over the next page of his note-book.

'Next we have Prendergast, and he is not so easy. I've not ignored the possibilities of Prendergast all through. He's an older man, and he's got both the brain and the will-power. There are certain good qualities, even if they're misdirected, which a man must have for a crime of this kind, and Prendergast has them. I don't believe that Mitton *could* commit a murder, but in certain circumstances Prendergast *might*. He's a deep man, and an able man, and a determined man, and so I've given a good deal of attention to his movements on Wednesday night. Listen. It's suspicious to begin with that it was he who first advanced the theory that one of those who dined at high table had committed the murder. Grant for a moment, and merely for the sake of argument, that he is the murderer. He guesses that sooner or later someone will point out that suspicion rests in the first instance on those who were dining; it is therefore sound policy for him to draw attention to the fact himself to avert suspicion from himself. Secondly he does not leave Common Room till ten o'clock. Why? Because everyone who goes out before him falls into the class of suspects if, as he hopes, each goes to his own rooms. Of course the time left to him is short. He has to run up and shoot Shirley before Hargreaves goes up himself to his rooms. But Hargreaves is deep in conversation at ten o'clock, and has apparently forgotten his appointment with Shirley. Prendergast can, then, probably count on ten minutes or a quarter of an hour. What does he do? He has to shoot Shirley and leave no trace, and of course his first thought is finger-prints. There are two ways in which a murderer can avoid them satisfactorily; either he can put on a pair of gloves, or he can wrap his handkerchief round his hand before he fires. But if you try the latter method you will find that it needs a little arrangement, and it has the drawback that the murderer may touch other objects with his hands after the crime has been committed. Now the fact that Shirley had apparently not moved in his chair points to the fact that the murderer picked up the

117

revolver and shot him almost before Shirley heard the door open. In other words, it is a fair assumption that the murderer used gloves and did not arrange a handkerchief round his hands. Do you agree?'

A nodded assent.

'Good. Then we can reconstruct Prendergast's movements, still on the assumption that he was the criminal. A man who had the nerve to wait till ten as he did would have his plans cut and dried. He walks straight to his rooms, takes a pair of gloves from his drawer, walks back to Hargreaves' rooms, pulls on the gloves as he mounts the stairs, opens the door of the inner room, picks up the revolver, shoots Shirley, and returns to his own rooms. If he meets anyone going up as he comes down he can give the alarm, and say that he has found Shirley shot; he's only in danger himself for about three minutes. With that possible reconstruction of events in my mind I did an old-fashioned piece of detection. I made friends with his servant, and asked him some questions. Candour, even if it was artificial candour, seemed the right line, so I boldly told him that the police had got it into their heads that the murderer had stolen a pair of gloves from someone in college in order to conceal finger-prints. Could he tell me if Mr Prendergast had missed any gloves from his drawer? He was interested at once, and did just what I had hoped he would – that is to say he took me straight up to Prendergast's bedroom (I must confess that I'd picked an hour when Prendergast was lecturing). He opened a drawer, and there were the gloves: – one pair of motoring gloves, much too thick and clumsy for the purpose, and three pairs of wash-leather gloves. But all the latter had been cleaned since they had been last used. You can't put on a pair of gloves without making it obvious that they had been used, and his servant was perfectly confident that Prendergast had no other gloves in his rooms. Indeed he possessed no other pair. So it's quite certain that if Prendergast did it he didn't do it in the way I described. And yet with his precision and nerve he *would* have done it in that way. He would have been sure that his gloves would have fitted him, and you want well-fitting gloves.'

More and more as he talked Brendel seemed to have half forgotten my presence; he spoke like a man arguing with himself, and gradually establishing his own conclusions.

'I can't say for certain that Prendergast did not do it,' he went on after a ruminative pause, 'but yet I'm almost sure that he didn't. Unless I've read his character all wrong he would have been an extraordinarily efficient murderer, if a murderer at all – and if competent, then he would have acted as I suggested – yet that he didn't do. I may have to come back to him, but for the time being I shall put him out of my mind. That leaves Mottram and Hargreaves alone out of all our original eight, and either of them might have been the murderer. Mottram is a retiring man, but there are hidden fires, or I am much mistaken. It is true that he went to his laboratory and that he was still there just after ten when his friend Holt visited him. But what was there to prevent him from coming down in his car, committing the murder, and returning? I've tried it in your car; he could have done the whole thing including the journey both ways in less than a quarter of an hour – and his alibi is only spasmodic. He's just as much under suspicion as ever he was. And Hargreaves too; I can find nothing which clears him. He was ten minutes alone in the Quad – so he says – before he went up to his rooms. Why didn't he go straight up to see Shirley? Isn't the explanation a little thin? But if he murdered Shirley at ten minutes past ten he might wait ten minutes before he returned in case even inexperienced persons like ourselves should realize that Shirley was only that moment dead. And then his character. I notice that you all tend to defer to Hargreaves, and to regard him as a person of importance, and yet somehow none of you really like him very much. Is he a little too sure of himself, a little overpowering, something of a bully – or is it only that you are jealous of him? I don't know, but I suspect that he is not quite the sound, reliable, good citizen that he likes to think himself. No, Hargreaves as well as Mottram is still on the list.'

I felt that it was time that I interrupted him.

'Really, Brendel,' I said, 'this wretched theory of yours and Prendergast's is destroying itself. It seems to show that the murderer must have been Mottram or Hargreaves, but by applying your own methods I can show that that is all nonsense. Mottram was the only man amongst us who was a genuine friend and well-wisher to Shirley, and that surely exonerates him. As for Maurice Hargreaves, he was on better terms with Shirley than most of us were, and besides, how could he have shot him in his own rooms? Flesh and blood couldn't stand that. Won't you admit that if he did mean to shoot Shirley for some reason of which we know nothing he'd have chosen any other place than his own room to do it in? No, no, it won't do. Believe me, you're barking up the wrong tree with Mottram and Hargreaves.'

'Even you, in this home of pure English! "Barking up the wrong tree" is admirable, and I thank you for it.'

I refused to be put off by his pleasantry.

'It seems to me quite certain that we have got to abandon Prendergast's theory, and start afresh. Theories are all very well, but we must be prepared to abandon them when they don't work out. Think of the improbability of anyone who dined that night shooting Shirley.'

Brendel shook his head ever so slightly.

'But consider the alternative! Are we to suppose that some enemy saw Shirley go up to Hargreaves' room, followed him there, found the revolver ready to his hand, and seized the opportunity? What a series of coincidences!

I've generally found, Winn, that, when the only alternatives are the improbable and the wildly improbable, it is wiser to concentrate on the former. However, we shall get no further by discussing that. Let's have a new list of suspects, for the old one is out of date. I insist·on putting Hargreaves and Mottram on it until you have adduced some evidence to clear them, and you would add an unknown X, whom we haven't yet got into touch with, isn't that so?'

I nodded.

'But there is one great difficulty, Winn, with regard to your unknown. He has to get into the college, and he has to get out again. If, as you would like to think, he's not a member of St Thomas's at all he has either to come in before nine o'clock, and hide himself somewhere, or else slip past your porter when he's not looking. Neither of those alternatives is an impossibility, but surely they're unlikely in the highest degree. And then again, having killed Shirley, the murderer has to secrete himself in college all through the night, or else run the gauntlet of the porter once again. Again I ask, is it likely? Wouldn't one of your lynx-eyed young men have noticed a stranger? Wouldn't someone have spoken to him? Of course there's the Fellows' door of which you spoke. Someone *may* have stolen a key, or even had a key made on purpose – but that at best is only a slender possibility, and there's no evidence to support it at all.'

'Just one thing,' I interrupted him. 'When I talked things over with Cotter we noticed that there was another way in, which you and I didn't discuss. I ought to have mentioned it before. You can come into the smaller Quadrangle through the President's Lodgings. Cotter took quite a lot of interest in the people who were in the Lodgings that night – I mean the servants and so forth.'

Brendel nodded appreciatively.

'Cotter is a competent man; of course he would notice

that. I also took some little interest in that door and in those people. Unless the butler there is lying no one entered the Lodgings that night except the President, his daughter, his two guests and the servants. But that doesn't exclude the possibility that one of them may have slipped out into the Quadrangle and visited Hargreaves' rooms. Well, X is a comprehensive symbol, and must include for the time being all unknowns whether they entered through the President's Lodgings or otherwise. That's three suspects, Hargreaves, Mottram, and X – and by the way, after our last additions, X may be a man or a woman – but there's still a fourth possibility.'

'Is there another?'

'Yes, and suggested by yourself in the first instance. Doesn't it occur to you that we have given very little attention to Callendar and his boy? Yet we know that they were both in possession of the important facts; they both knew where Shirley had gone, they both probably knew where the revolver lay. And that boy is very much awake too, as you have reason to know. Why shouldn't one of them have done it, or even, why shouldn't they have been in collusion? One might have shot Shirley whilst the other watched to see that the coast was clear. We know of no motive, it is true, but we do not in any of the other cases. Besides, you probably know less about their thoughts and feelings than about those of your colleagues.'

He looked at me to see what impression his words had made. I felt puzzled how to reply.

'Callendar is an old and trusted servant of the college,' I began, but Brendel interrupted me with, I thought, unnecessary haste.

'Yes, yes, and Hargreaves is a respected and trusted Dean, but that's not the point. Callendar might have done it, just as, in the present state of our knowledge, Hargreaves might have. Anyhow, think over the new list of suspects.'

Twelve o'clock began to strike as he spoke, and he got up to go.

'I will certainly,' I said, 'but you may be quite sure that X is the only one on your new list who is ever likely to hang for the murder of Shirley.'

# CHAPTER THIRTEEN

EVERY man has his special foible; my own was a harmless
one, which had for many years given me a good deal of quiet
pleasure. I had made it my boast that I could tell the
character of any visitor in general outline by the nature of
his knock on my door. An amiable weakness, no doubt, and
a claim not susceptible of very accurate demonstration,
but still it had provided me with much innocent amusement. My rooms were well adapted for the exercise of what
I had come to look upon as my special gift. As is often the
case at Oxford my oak, or outer door, opened into a small
lobby, leading from which were two more doors, the one
giving admittance to the larger of my two sitting-rooms, the
other to my bedroom. A stranger, entering this lobby, was
wont to pause irresolutely before the two doors, and this
fact made his knock, when at length it came, especially
instructive to me. If it was hesitating and self-exculpatory,
I immediately translated it in some such words as these:
'I trust that I have not knocked at the wrong door; if this
is your bedroom, pray forgive me,' and I pictured to myself
an individual timid and self-effacing. The pause too which
elapsed between the arrival and the first knock was of
great importance. A visitor of quick decision would soon
make his choice of doors and put the matter to the test;
one of cautious temperament would hesitate much longer
before he made up his mind. I had even once been able to
add to my collection a stranger so diffident and yet so
anxious to do right that he had knocked simultaneously on
both doors, on one with his right, on the other with his left
hand. But many of my visitors gave information to me
by their knocks of quite another kind. There was the
angry knocker who, after a very brief pause, would strike
loudly on one door or the other, as though he meant to say,

'I really don't care if this is the right door or not, but damn you all the same for leaving me in doubt!' When such a knock came I diagnosed an egotist of the dominating type, and braced myself for an unpleasant interview. Sometimes again the knock would announce to me criticism of a more patient though equally disapproving kind, and I would guess a business man, or one of those self-chosen organizers and reformers, saying with his knuckles, 'What an inefficient arrangement; why in Heaven's name don't you have a card pinned up to tell me which to choose?' Such deductions were only the A B C of my art; with my academic friends and pupils my technique was much more advanced. Undergraduates, I was wont to maintain, changed their methods from year to year. A freshman's knock was usually shy and apologetic; it seemed to say, 'I'm compelled to do this, but perhaps I may be lucky enough to find you out – if so I shall waste no time in retiring.' Quite different the second-year man's rather noisy summons! 'If anyone owns this college, it's probably I and my friends; I've brought up some work for you – not a great deal, but quite as much as you're entitled to expect – you may criticize it if you like, but I don't mind much what you say, and anyhow life is a pleasant thing at my age, and I can't waste too much time over my tutor.' The third-year man again would knock quite differently. My interpretation in his case was something after this kind. 'Are you in? If so, please reply without delay. The schools are getting near, and I have no time to waste. It would be useful to discuss things with you, and I should like to get to business quickly, so please cut out unnecessary preliminaries.' The fourth-year man or the B.A. again had his own special method. His was the knock of a man who had learned how to use his time well, and yet had no need of excessive haste. 'Are you in?' he would say. 'If so I shall be glad to have some conversation with you. I come as an intellectual equal to discuss subjects in which we have a common interest. I hope for your sake, as well as mine, that you are at home and disengaged.' Those who visited me often, of course, I could name before ever they entered my room. Mitton had a more apologetic knock than even the most callow of freshmen; when I heard him I used to think of a spinster district visitor uncertain of her reception. He seemed to be saying, 'Could you be so very kind as to admit me for a few moments? I really won't stay longer, and whatever you do don't get up from your chair or put yourself out in any way.' How different was Hargreaves! His knock was that of the successful, dominating, almost bullying person, and it always exasperated me. It seemed to betoken a man who neither expected delay nor tolerated opposition, who assumed as a matter of course that his presence would be welcome and that everything and everyone else would wait on his convenience. The arrival of Trower was heralded by a terrific bombardment on the panels of my door. In early life he had taken part in military operations in Ashanti and other parts of Africa, and I always supposed that he had acquired there habits which he found it impossible to shake off. Savage chieftains, who had heard lions roaring by night, or gorillas drumming on their chests, or elephants trumpeting in the forest, might yet, I felt, have surrendered at discretion if Trower had thundered at the entrance of their huts. Even Doyne, who was in the room, like a draught of fresh air, before I had time to say 'Come in,' was mild in his methods of knocking compared to Trower. As for Shirley, he used to enter without knocking at all, a habit for which I had never been able to excuse him.

A sure instinct warned me that I was not likely to be long undisturbed on Monday morning. I had hardly lit my after-breakfast pipe, and prepared to diagnose my first knock, when it came. 'No academic knuckles, those,' was my immediate mental note. The knock was business-like and incisive. It said in effect, 'Are you in? If so, I have business to discuss with you, which is important and for which I require your attention.' There was even a hint of menace. 'I shall take careful note of all you say, so be careful.' I guessed Cotter, and said, 'Come in.' My guess was correct.

The Inspector wasted no time; he accepted a chair and refused a cigarette.

'I need your help again, Sir,' he began. 'This case is not going well – in fact it's not going at all. The line of investigation through Mr Scarborough was no use; he burned his hand that night, and couldn't have fired the shot; the evidence of your Head Porter clears him entirely.'

'Exactly,' I said rather incautiously.

'Did you know that?' he asked suspiciously.

I hastened to clear myself of the implied charge of having again withheld information from the Inspector.

'I only heard it late last night,' I explained, 'long after we'd had our talk, and too late to let you know. But I'm glad that he's no longer suspected.'

Cotter nodded. 'Yes. His alibi is all right. But I can't get a start anywhere; there's still no clue, and I can't even put together a reasonable theory to account for the crime. I even considered at one time the possibility that the murderer might have intended to shoot Mr Hargreaves and then shot Mr Shirley by mistake. But in that light it hardly seems possible that the murderer could have mistaken one head for the other over the top of the chair, however quickly he fired. And besides it doesn't help me a bit, for there's even less motive to allege in that case than in the other. No one seems to have liked Mr Shirley, but Mr Hargreaves is apparently a very popular person. I'm up against a brick wall, and that's the truth. I've cross-examined practically everyone who was in the college that night, and I can't find any clue whatever. It seems to me that there's only one thing to do. I *must* find some suggestion of motive, something to give me a start, and so I want you to talk again to everyone closely connected with Mr Shirley. I can't get anything out of his widow, and still less from his father-in-law, but you may be able to. Will you try them again, and go over every little detail in his life, and his acquaintances, and his affairs? Something must surely turn up which will give me a start.'

'I'll try, of course,' I said doubtfully, 'but I don't feel much confidence in the result. Still, I'll do my best.'

Cotter thanked me, and got up.

'If nothing new turns up this is going to be one of the great unexplained mysteries,' he remarked gloomily, 'and I shan't exactly gain much in reputation from it.'

He had hardly left me when I heard a knock which by now I knew well, for it was Brendel's. It was firm and reassuring, but without a hint of aggression. To me its message had come to be, 'I hope you are in, for I should like a talk with you, and I think I may be helpful to you.' My 'Come in' was therefore prompt and cordial.

When I had told him of Cotter's visit, and of the latter's pessimistic outlook, he smiled, and warned me to go warily with my questions to Mrs Shirley. I was already conscious that I had undertaken rather lightly a difficult and not very agreeable task, and I began to wish that I had declined it. Brendel, however, quieted my doubts, and said that he was confident that my tact would smooth out the difficulties. He then asked me about the funeral arrangements for that day.

I explained to him what had been arranged; there was to be a service in the chapel at two o'clock, and the second part of the service would follow at the cemetery. To my great surprise he showed the keenest interest in all the details, and I had to tell him whom it was proposed to admit, and who would in all probability go on to the cemetery. Shirley was a man of few friends, but the President had been nervous lest the vulgar excitement caused by his death should attract a crowd, and we had therefore settled that except for members of the college, who would naturally attend, and a few relatives, no one should be admitted to the chapel except by a special permit. We anticipated that only the relatives and the Fellows of the college would follow the body to the cemetery.

'I should like to go to both parts of the service,' said Brendel when I had finished; 'will there be any objection?'

'None, of course, but no one could possibly think it incumbent on you to attend, unless you wish it.'

He smiled a little wryly.

'The detective can't always be over-nice in his methods. I don't want to deceive you about my intentions. I go to the funeral because I want to watch some of the mourners. And so that I may watch well may I now see your chapel, and learn where they will all sit?'

I could not pretend to like the idea of using a funeral service for such a purpose, but I could hardly press my objection, which was in fact one of sentiment rather than of reason, so I made a virtue of necessity and walked down with Brendel towards the chapel.

As we crossed the Quad, the porter hurried across the path and handed me a telegram. I opened it and found that one of my minor worries was at an end, for it was from Fred Scarborough, and ran as follows: 'Have burned your letter unread. Are you all mad at St Thomas's? Shall expect the whole story later.' I showed it to Brendel, and then led the way into the chapel.

Our chapel was an eighteenth-century addition to the college, of no great size, but perfectly proportioned and beautiful both in design and decoration. It was rectangular in shape, with long pews, dark with age, running in three rows along each side. The organ was at the west end, on one side of the entrance, and opposite it, on the other side, was a small vestry. Brendel was not blind to the beauties of the building, which he examined with care and with aesthetic appreciation. But he was even more interested in the practical details of seating and accommodation.

'I think I understand,' he said, when I had concluded my explanations. 'The whole of the undergraduates sit at the east end on both sides of the chapel; and those seats at the west end are reserved for the Fellows. The rows behind the Fellows' seats, are they at the disposal of visitors?'

'Yes.'

'You say that the Fellows sit on both sides of the chapel; has each a special seat, or does each sit where he will?'

'The President and Vice-President – that is myself – have our special seats, and of course the Chaplain, but the rest have not.'

'But do the others in practice usually sit in the same places?'

'Well, as a matter of fact, most of them hardly ever come; when they do they sit sometimes on one side and sometimes on the other. Trower always takes that corner seat, because he likes to read the lessons, but the rest, I fancy, chop and change.'

'I see. Now may I sit in a back pew, on either side, whichever I choose?'

'Certainly. There won't be a crowd, for we've taken steps, as I told you, to keep out strangers. I think you are sure to find room on whichever side you like.'

He made another careful survey of the chapel, and I could not help feeling that he was wasting a good deal of time over a very trivial matter, but I knew better than to point out this to him. Finally, he seemed satisfied and we left the chapel.

*

The rest of the morning seemed interminable to me. I had pupils to teach, but I found it impossible to concentrate my mind upon their work. I could think of nothing but the unexplained mystery, and Shirley's body lying in its coffin.

*

It was almost with a sense of relief that at last I found myself seated in my pew in chapel, waiting for the service to begin.

Brendel came in at the last moment. I saw him give a long unhurried look at the congregation, first on one side and then on the other, before he moved to a vacant seat two or three places from me on the north side of the chapel. Hardly had he seated himself when he bent across and murmured some words into the ear of a cousin of Shirley's, who was sitting almost next to me, in the same row as Brendel. I thought I caught the words 'rather deaf ... don't hear at all well ... mind if I change places?' and apparently I was not deceived, for the other man nodded, and he and Brendel rapidly changed places. I had not time to speculate about Brendel's remark, which I knew to be quite untrue, for at that moment the service began.

I had come to chapel with a sense almost of relief, but my mood soon changed to one of unrelieved gloom and misery. Like most normal men I hold all funerals in abhorrence, those at Oxford more especially. The long black gowns, the wearing of which on such occasions is imposed upon us by University traditions, gave the ceremony an appearance which is macabre as well as funereal. The contrast between the rows of youthful undergraduate faces at one end of the chapel and the senior members of the University, many of them old and bent, at the other, seemed to emphasize the shortness and precarious nature of human life, whilst the unrelieved black of the congregation and the haunting sadness of the music filled me with a depression that I could barely conceal. I felt anew the pain and grief of the wife of the murdered man and of her sister, the two people whom of all my acquaintance I most loved and reverenced; I saw as it seemed even without looking in his direction the figure of the white-haired President, bowed and broken in spirit. For the first time I realized the whole horror of what had occurred; for the first time I faced the knowledge that life at St Thomas's could never be the same as it had been before the shadow of crime had fallen upon the college. It seemed to me as though happiness had been blotted out from the lives of those whom I most cherished, and that my own life was involved in the common ruin. I had never had any real affection for Shirley himself, but his murder seemed at that moment to be the death-knell of my own quiet happiness. Up to then in some curious way I had felt that the events which had suddenly disturbed the whole tenor of our collegiate life had been external to myself. I had watched them as a spectator, even when I had been participating in them. I had felt all the time as though in some miraculous way things would suddenly be restored to the state in which they had been before the murder; that I should resume my old life of ease and contentment; that the dark clouds of crime and tragedy would suddenly disperse. But now at last I realized the inevitability of what had happened, and I felt the whole load of irremediable misery. Others, I think, must have suffered in the same way; even those of my colleagues who had discussed the crime as though it had been a mere problem in crime and detection, seemed now to feel that indeed it impinged upon their own lives.

The second part of the service at the cemetery was almost unbearable. A light rain had begun to fall, and dripped miserably upon the small crowd of persons round the open grave. At one moment I feared that Mary, who stood facing me, was going to faint, so desperately pale and ill did she look. The same thought seemed to occur to Mottram, who was standing near to her, for I saw his arm stretched out for a moment to support her. But she seemed to recover almost immediately, and Mottram's arm fell back to his side. Slowly the rain increased; the atmosphere was one of inspissated gloom. Short though it was it seemed to me that the service would never end. But at last it was over, and the cars drove us slowly back again to St Thomas's.

*

It was a dismal home-coming. I paced up and down my room in a state of acute depression, and a prey as usual to wretched indecision. Should I, or should I not, go to the Verekers' that evening? I longed to lend them what help and sympathy I could, and I felt sure that a visit from me would never be considered in that house as an intrusion; but I could not make up my mind to go. Might I not do more harm than good, if I tried to find words of sympathy and comfort?

About half-past five I could bear my own company and my own thoughts no longer. There are times when human society of some kind is an absolute necessity. I had decided that I would not go to the Verekers', but with some human being I must converse. Almost by chance I decided to go to see if Mottram was in his rooms. What guided me there I cannot say, for he was a man whom I seldom visited; probably it was the fact that I had a mental picture of him standing opposite to me at the graveside. Be that how it may, I found myself walking across to the back Quad, and mounting his staircase.

As I approached I heard voices, but I paid no special attention to them, for my mind was full of its own thoughts. I knocked and entered, without waiting for a reply. It happened, therefore, that I was actually in the room before its occupants were aware of my presence, so absorbed were they in their conversation. The scene which met my eyes has imprinted itself indelibly upon my memory. Mottram stood upright on one side of the fireplace, his whole body quivering with emotion, his mouth grimly set, his eyes fixed with an almost savage intensity upon his companion. So, as it seemed to me, must an ancient prophet have looked as he cursed his country's enemies. But if his appearance startled me, still more did that of his companion, for on the other side of the fireplace sat Maurice Hargreaves – not the Maurice Hargreaves whom I knew, not the confident, self-assertive, dominating man of action and decision, but a person who seemed to me somehow to be exploded – shrunken and contemptible like a man who has been found out and exposed to public shame. The attitudes of the two men, the expressions on their faces, the atmosphere of the room, which I sensed at the very moment that I entered it, all told the same story. There had been a quarrel and Mottram had been the aggressor; a struggle and Mottram had prevailed. Hargreaves, who always had his way, had, for some inexplicable reason, been worsted and humiliated. He was trying now, but not very successfully, to control his feelings and minimize the extent of his defeat. As they became suddenly aware of my presence there was a swift, uncomfortable, unreal silence, and then Maurice appeared to pull himself together. He got up from his chair, muttered, 'That's all, I think – good night, Mottram,' nodded to me, and walked out of the room.

I made a desperate effort to pass things off lightly. 'By Jove, Mottram,' I said, 'you do look excited. Really I might have thought just now that you knew some dreadful secret about Maurice and had just told him so.'

He gave me a queer, almost savage look.

'Perhaps I do,' he said.

His answer gave me a new and even more alarming shock, and for a moment I could hardly grasp his meaning. As its implications dawned on me I felt a little faint, and I steadied myself against the table.

'For pity's sake be careful, Mottram, as to what you say. At a time when the whole place is under the shadow of a crime a remark like that is a terrible accusation. You say that you know some dreadful secret – or at least you don't deny that you know it – about Maurice. Are you really telling me that he is a murderer? You've gone so far that you must tell me all you know, but I implore you not to say anything that you can't substantiate.'

He gave a curious grating laugh.

'No, Winn, I didn't say that Hargreaves was a murderer; of course he's not; but . . . I can't and won't tell you anything more now.'

Suddenly he gripped me by the arm, and looked straight into my eyes.

'I've said too much already; I ought never to have done that, but you surprised me. But promise me one thing; wait three days; forget what I said till then. I beg you to do that; I give you my word that no harm will be done to any human being if you wait so long. After that inquire what you will. But promise me to wait till then.'

There was an intensity of emotion in his voice that I could hardly resist, but I shook my head. 'I can't promise that,' I said; 'I must have time to think. But I will go this far; I promise to tell what you have said to one other person only, and to be guided by his advice. If he agrees I will do as you wish.'

Mottram shrugged his shoulders; his excitement seemed to have deserted him suddenly, and left him limp and nerveless.

'Thank you,' he said, 'but I believe that you may regret it all your life if you don't wait and keep your counsel.'

From Mottram's rooms I hurried to Brendel's, and found to my intense relief that he was in and alone.

'What am I to do?' I asked when I had put him in possession of the facts. 'Mottram tells me in a momentary burst of confidence that he is in possession of some secret about Hargreaves; the whole appearance and demeanour of Hargreaves suggest that that secret is indeed a shameful if not a dangerous one; it stands to reason that it must have some close connexion with the murder. Yet almost in the same breath Mottram begs me not to attempt to follow up this inquiry for three days. That must be madness, but what am I to do?'

Brendel thought for a considerable time before he answered, and when he did he spoke with unusual care, and very seriously.

'I cannot pretend to control your actions, my dear Winn, in any way whatever. You are a free agent, and must decide this for yourself. But if you ask me as a friend what I should do in your place I will reply quite candidly. I should do precisely what Mottram asked you to do. Yes, I believe that you would regret it if you took any course but that.'

It was not the advice which I had expected, and I did not for a moment feel satisfied, yet I knew that I should follow it. For Brendel seemed to assume responsibility, and I, for my part, was only too glad to feel that he had done so.

# CHAPTER FOURTEEN

IF the day of Shirley's funeral had appeared to me the longest day of my life, the two which immediately followed it seemed an eternity. And they seemed all the more wretched because, to my impatient mind, those most concerned gave the impression of doing little or nothing to elucidate the mystery. Like many a man of slightly infirm purpose – and of such in moments of introspection I sometimes allowed myself to be – I was prone in times of crisis to demand with fussy insistence that something should be done. Conscious of the truth of Lord Melbourne's classic warning to such as myself I yet contrived at such times always to forget it. Unable to act myself I was tireless in urging others to action. So now with the passing of each leaden hour I felt that opportunities were being wasted, which would never return. Why was Brendel sitting idle while the scent grew cold? Why was not Cotter still rushing from one person to another, questioning, exploring, tracking down the culprit? I had an absurd feeling that the whole college was being lulled or even hypnotized into a state of acquiescence in failure. The official view, shared by most of my colleagues, had come to be that some person unknown, and as yet unsuspected, *must* have been the murderer, since no one within the college could, on reflexion, be seriously suspected. With that view I was inclined to agree – or had been until the time of my interview with Mottram – but whether it was right or wrong I fumed and fretted at the thought of leaving it unproved. Would Cotter really leave us, confessing that this mystery was as dark as when he was first consulted? And Brendel, who had said at the beginning that he was afraid of what he would find, would he go away having found out exactly nothing? His last lecture was to be delivered on the

Wednesday, and I knew that he planned to return to Vienna at the end of the week. Did he propose to sit with hands folded until then, and take leave of us without contributing anything towards a solution? That would be deception indeed. I had trusted in him, and he was going to fail me, like everyone else. Why had he tamely agreed to Mottram's request for delay, when action was imperatively called for? Was not the obvious explanation that he saw no possibility of success in his quest, and meant to leave us to our troubles with a minimum of annoyance to himself? My mood throughout these days did not remain constant. When I chanced to meet Brendel I felt almost at once the warm glow of trust which his presence and voice always produced in me; how could I have doubted him, so wise, so confident, so sure? Yet once more alone I would sink back into doubt and perplexity and self-pity. The revelation of my own weakness and incompetence reduced me to a pitiful state of nervous discomfort. So must many, I reflected, of those great historical figures have suffered about whom I had so often glibly lectured and whom I had often castigated for their indecisions – themselves too feeble, or events too great.

The slow torture of those days was on Wednesday afternoon made almost unbearable by an incident which was to me indescribably distressing, and which I was totally at a loss to explain. Ever since the funeral I had been screwing up my courage to call upon the Verekers, partly because I wanted to offer my sympathy to them, partly because I was pledged to Cotter to attempt to gain some more information. I had indeed decided to call on the Tuesday afternoon, but I had learned that the President had wisely enough taken both his daughters away for the whole day into the country to visit his sister, and so I had had perforce to wait – but on Wednesday I could evade my responsibilities no longer. About four o'clock I chanced to see

Ruth and Mary enter the President's Lodgings together, and so, about ten minutes later, I myself knocked on the door.

The President's butler, whom I had known for thirty years, opened it, but, instead of greeting me with his usual smile of welcome, compounded of exactly the right amount of dignity and respect, and an intimation that the ladies were in the drawing-room, told me in an embarrassed manner that neither Mrs Shirley nor Miss Vereker could receive any visitors.

'But, Hanbury,' I said, 'I'm not a visitor in the ordinary sense of the term. I feel quite certain that they would wish to see *me*. Just go back and tell Miss Vereker who is here, and I feel sure that she will be glad if I come in.'

Hanbury went away to do my bidding, though I could see that he felt uneasy. In a few moments he returned. Miss Vereker was very sorry, but she and her sister were unable to see anyone that afternoon.

I left the house feeling bitterly humiliated, and more miserable than ever before in my life. For thirty years that door had never been closed to me; I had watched Ruth and Mary grow up – I had been their friend and counsellor and confidant. From them I had received kindness and help unstintedly; they had prevented me from loneliness as I grew older, they had cheered me into good temper when I was bored or fretful. And in return I had given them both all that I had to give of sympathy and devotion. Yet now, when they must most need their friends, I found myself turned away and rejected. In what had I offended? Could Brendel's untimely questions have so hurt them that I too, as his friend, was under a cloud? Had I fallen short of my duty to them in any way? I returned to my lonely rooms, a prey to the most harassing and depressing thoughts. That night I could not face the company of my colleagues. I dined alone in my rooms, and after dinner sat for some hours in my chair, pretending to read, but in fact turning the events of the last week over and over in my mind, as I sought desperately but vainly for some clue which should guide me to an explanation of the mystery of Shirley's murder.

*

Events happen when they are least expected. I had resigned myself to another day of helpless misery, and was wondering how I should bring my mind to its task of the day's teaching, as I idly turned over the leaves of *The Times* on Thursday morning. And then suddenly an announcement caught and held my astonished eyes. It ran as follows: 'The marriage arranged between Maurice Hargreaves, Fellow and Dean of St Thomas's College, Oxford, and Miss Mary Vereker will not take place.'

My first reaction was one of blazing anger and disgust. Unfavourably though I had sometimes estimated Maurice's character I could never have credited him with an act of such callous cruelty as this. To break off his engagement at such a time, or even to allow Mary to break it! That, at a time when she was tortured by trouble and racked with the wretched details of a hateful tragedy, seemed to me inhuman. No explanation seemed reasonable, no excuse possible. I had always thought of Maurice as a gentleman, even when I had most disliked him, now I could only feel that he was a cad, for whom no words could be harsh enough. I sprang from my chair, and paced up and down the room, considering what could be done to protect Mary from this new disaster. So distraught was I that I did not hear Brendel's knock, and only observed him when he stood before me.

'Have you seen this – this damnable thing?' I asked, pushing *The Times* into his hands.

'Yes,' he replied; 'half an hour ago, and I'm not altogether surprised. Don't be carried off your feet, Winn.

There is more in this than appears on the surface, but I hope you'll be patient for a little while, and not try to put things right in a hurry. Meantime I've a request to make.'

I was altogether surprised both by his manner and his remarks. The seeming lethargy of the day before had deserted him; he was all briskness and decision, but his face was unsmiling.

'What do you want?'

'I want to borrow your car for the whole day. The sun is shining almost for the first day since I came here, and I mean to spend the whole day out on the Berkshire Downs. Can I have it? I have just made Mottram promise to come with me.'

My surprise changed to astonishment, but I could only consent to what seemed to me a rather extraordinary request.

'And the crime,' I hazarded, 'is there nothing to be done about that? Are we to go on sitting still and doing nothing?'

He patted me sympathetically on the shoulder.

'You must let me go my own way, please. But tell me this: Are you dining out this evening?'

'Indeed no. I should be poor company indeed. I'd intended to dine in Hall as usual, but I'm not sure that I can face even that if Maurice Hargreaves is going to be there.'

'Then do dine in Hall to please me, and keep yourself free after dinner. I think that I shall have something, and perhaps a great deal, to tell you then. We are very near to the end of this trail.'

Before I could question him further he was gone, and I sat down more mystified than ever to continue my ruminations.

*

Thursday seemed indeed interminable. Men of infirm

purpose always tend in my experience to comfort themselves with catchwords and quotations. There is a false
sense of finality and decision about the *ex cathedra* statements
of the great and the utterances of literary persons. I used
often to feel in argument or discussion in Common Room
that I had decided the question at issue when I had found
some apposite citation which seemed to sum up my view.
And yet, in reality, how useless and barren such things
are! That day, I remember, Swinburne's words went
echoing and re-echoing through my head:

> *From too much love of living,*
> *From hope and fear set free,*
> *We thank with brief thanksgiving*
> *Whatever gods may be*
> *That no life lives for ever;*
> *That dead men rise up never;*
> *That even the weariest river*
> *Winds somewhere safe to sea.*

Cold comfort at the best!

And yet for all that time did seem to stand still, and I
thought that the evening would never come.

\*

When at long last I made my way towards Common Room
just before seven-thirty I found Brendel waiting for me. He
drew me aside, and spoke with urgency.

'Listen. I want you to stay in Common Room until ten
o'clock. After that I have promised Mottram something.
Don't be surprised. You and I are to go up in your car
to the laboratory to fetch him from there. Is that all right?'

'But he's got his own car, and it's rather ridiculous to go
out at that time for nothing.'

'Never mind. I know it's unusual, but that doesn't
matter. If anyone asks you, say that I am interested in
Mottram's work, or anything else you like. But at ten

o'clock we go up together to the laboratory. *Sie müssen auf alle Fälle mitkommen.*'

I knew that he was worried from the fact that he had dropped unconsciously into German, but I had no opportunity for further discussion, for the other diners were already collecting. I nodded acquiescence and we moved together up to Hall.

Conversation that evening was perfunctory and spasmodic. Everyone was ill at ease, and although Maurice Hargreaves was not with us no one, not even Doyne, seemed anxious to discuss the announcement which we had all seen in *The Times*. By half past nine nobody was left by the Common Room fire except Brendel and myself, and between us, for the first time since our acquaintance had begun, conversation halted. Brendel was palpably ill at ease. Though as a rule the most finished and appreciative of smokers he allowed an expensive cigar to go out half-smoked and then threw it almost petulantly into the fire. He interspersed lengthy periods of silence with feverish bursts of disconnected remarks; he paced the room as though some form of activity were a physical necessity to him. And yet, as ten o'clock approached, he showed no desire to leave.

'A little longer; it will be difficult; give him a little longer,' he muttered more to himself than to me, and it was not until about five minutes past ten that, after looking at his watch for the twentieth time, he suddenly seemed to make a decision.

'We must go now,' he said; 'come and get the car. We put on our greatcoats and walked by way of the Fellows' door to the open space behind the college where my car was parked. I opened the door to step into the driver's seat, but Brendel laid a restraining hand on my arm.

'I think I'll drive, if you don't mind,' he said. I was

surprised and no doubt my face showed it. I am by no means an expert driver, indeed it was a standing joke among my younger colleagues that I combined a maximum of risk with a minimum of speed, but still Brendel's suggestion piqued me, for we had, after all, only a five-minute drive before us through almost empty streets.

He guessed what was passing in my mind, and hastened to correct the false impression which his remark had made.

'It's not that, Winn. I'm not so pusillanimous as you think me. But I've got something which must be told you as we drive up, and I want your whole attention.'

Nothing could have been more friendly than the words, but where was that smile which I had come to expect and to enjoy? Brendel's face was hard and expressionless, as though he had forced it into a rigid mask. The disquiet which had been growing on me during the evening turned to something almost like panic, and I braced myself to meet some new and as yet unknown disaster.

Brendel started the car, and we moved off in the direction of the laboratory, but it was not until we were already half-way to our destination that he suddenly spoke.

'Winn, I can't let you go quite unprepared. I think – I'm not quite sure – but I think that when we arrive we shall . . . not find Mottram alive.' I had expected bad news of some kind, but the words when they came were like a knock-out blow.

'For God's sake tell me what you mean. Is there some other horrible tragedy? What is it all about?'

Brendel bent his head lower over the wheel as he replied, and his voice was very grave.

'I can't tell you more till we get there, and after all I may be wrong, but I couldn't let you enter that room without letting you know first what you might find. I believe that we shall find that Mottram has taken his life.'

Wild thoughts raced through my mind. Why, in Heaven's

name, if this was true, had we sat for the last two hours with hands folded in the Common Room? Had Brendel for some unfathomable reason wished as well as foreseen this second tragedy? And what bearing, if any, had it on Shirley's death? Such were the questions which were on the tip of my tongue, but I could not ask them. I waited helplessly till I should know whether this new disaster was hard fact or idle fancy.

As we drew up by the door of the laboratory I noticed that the windows of the room where Mottram worked were alight, whilst the rest of the building was in darkness; apparently there were no other workers there that night. Brendel, I think, made the same observation, for he cast a rapid glance over the exterior of the building, and nodded his head as though satisfied. Then he produced a key from his pocket, and opened the main door. Like an automaton I followed him. I had a curious sensation as though I were acting in a play; my movements seemed to me to have been dictated to me, and I carried them out without conscious volition on my part. And all the while terror gripped me; a growing certainty that in the next minute I should once more be face to face with tragedy and death.

Brendel seemed to know his way well over the building. He switched on a light in the passage, and led me without hesitation to Mottram's room. Then he knocked once, firmly, on the door.

There was no answer.

Brendel knocked again, but I knew, as he must have, that no reply would come. Then, after the briefest pause, he tried the handle of the door. It did not open, but he pulled another key from his pocket, and unlocked it.

I think that the worst horror of the evening was over before I crossed the threshold, for now I saw only what in my mind's eye I had already seen – and flinched from. Mottram was in a chair, half lying, half sitting, and I knew long before I looked at his face that he was dead. In front of him on a shelf was an empty glass and two envelopes, one very bulky and the other of ordinary size. As I looked at these I noticed with surprise that the larger was addressed to me.

Brendel, meantime, had felt Mottram's heart and satisfied himself that he was dead; then he bent over the empty glass and smelt it.

'Prussic acid. I thought so,' he muttered. He walked back to the door and carefully locked it.

'I don't think we shall be disturbed,' he said; 'but it's as well to be certain. You'd better open that letter, and see what's in it. Perhaps you might read it aloud.'

Of a sudden I felt rather faint, and sat down abruptly in a chair.

'Oughtn't we to send for the police first?' I asked.

'I don't think so; there is nothing to be done for him now, and I believe that the letter should be read before we decide what to do.'

I opened the large envelope obediently and pulled out a dozen closely written sheets of manuscript. I had thought that Brendel had remained almost inhumanly calm, but I noticed, as he too pulled up a chair, that his hand trembled ever so little.

'I think, Winn,' he said very gently, 'that you are going to read the life history of a man, whom you have lived with for eight years and never known.'

# CHAPTER FIFTEEN

The early part of Mottram's letter was full of erasures and corrections and made up of short, jerky sentences, as though he had found it difficult to express his meaning, but I saw, as I glanced at the manuscript in my hands, that, after he had once got fairly under way, he had poured out a spate of words without pausing to alter or elaborate them. Evidently he had made up his mind after an initial struggle to tell his tale without restraint or inhibition. The letter began abruptly without any kind of introduction. I have set it down just as it was written.

'I am a murderer, though God knows that I never meant to kill Shirley. Brendel knows most of this story, but not all. I write it down for you, Winn, because I have no friend to turn to, and that perhaps is the source of all the trouble. Someone must know it all before I go. I beg of you to read to the end, and to try to understand. It means going back to the beginning, but I can't help that. For I *must* make you understand, and that is the only way.

'You know, I think, that both my parents died when I was quite small. I lived with an uncle; he wasn't unkind to me, but he just didn't care. There was hardly any money; just enough to pay for my schooling, and that was all. Always it was dinned into my head that at the earliest opportunity I must earn my own living. I think my uncle hoped to see me a clerk in a bank, and then to wash his hands of me. I don't blame him; he was always ill and I was nothing to him but a burden and a responsibility. I went to a Grammar School in the north; it wasn't a good school, and the teaching was generally pretty bad. But there were a couple of masters who were better than the average and somehow I learned to work. How I worked! Partly, I suppose, because I had nothing else to do, and no chance of amusing myself, but more because I loved it, and more still because I saw in work a way of escape from the life which my uncle had planned for me. I spoiled my health, and I ruined my eyesight, but what did that matter? Somehow I won scholarships and prizes, enough to take me to the University. And that is how I came to Oxford. I won enough money to bring me here – just enough and no more.

'At Oxford it was the same story. I worked day and night, but I was starved for friendship. Partly I couldn't afford to have friends, partly I hadn't the time for them, partly I hadn't the knack of making them. I was obsessed with the idea that I would carve out a great career for myself in medicine, and then pick up all the other things I'd missed. But you can't do it that way. If you postpone pleasures you never taste them. In a sort of way again I succeeded. Everyone prophesied great things for me; they said that I'd done better work in the schools than anyone for the last twenty years, and when I was elected to your research fellowship at St Thomas's I thought that at last I had reached the end of a long trail, and that the good days would begin. I saw a vista of happy and well-filled days, of congenial society and steady friendships, and of work which would bring me recognition and fame and con-tentment.

'It didn't work out like that. You weren't unkind to me, but no one seemed to care. I suppose it was my fault. I'd lost or wasted all the human contacts I might have had, and I just didn't know how to set about making friends. I can never forget my first night in Common Room. Half the table was discussing a political novel which had just been published, and I had never heard the author's name, much less those of the people about whom he wrote; Hargreaves was discussing cricket, and I had never seen or even wished to see a first-class match; Shepardson was speaking of wine, and I could not tell a claret from a burgundy. All your interests and your conversation and even your jokes were strange and alien and incomprehensible to me. One by one you tried to draw me into conversation, and one by one you gave me up. I was a member of Common Room, but I might just as well not have been there, for all the difference my presence made. I blame no one; you all had your language and it wasn't mine. So I became lonelier than ever. Of course I ought to have gone out into the world, but I wanted to conquer in my own way. I determined that in my laboratory I would triumph. There at least I was master of my fate, there I might win distinction which would make me someone in the world at last. And so I worked harder than ever before.

'There was one exception to the general indifference. I refused the first two invitations which came to me from the President's Lodgings because I was too shy and too self-conscious to accept them, but I couldn't decently refuse the third. Ruth wrote to me the sort of note which made a refusal impossible. "I do hope you will come this time," she said, "for my sister and I can't bear to think that there is a Fellow of St Thomas's whom we've never even met. It's not a party – there will only be my father and ourselves – so please say Yes." I went because I had to, but I found what I had always wanted – understanding and friendship, and sympathy. They saw at once that I had no small talk and very few interests, and so they talked about my work and about the medical school and also about themselves. And somehow they made me talk too. For the first time I didn't feel shut out.

'I think I fell in love with Ruth the first time I entered that house; I knew that I was deeply, irrevocably, in love with her before my first term here was over. Did she know or guess? I can't tell. Perhaps I was never anything more to her than the dim little research Fellow with clumsy manners and no conversation, to whom she was kind because I belonged to St Thomas's, and because she was kind by nature. But she changed my whole world for me, and I began to dream dreams of a future so happy that I hardly dared to contemplate it. Then the blow fell. I'd been here more than two years when Ruth became engaged to Shirley, and I'd never suspected that she even liked him. When I heard the news it seemed as though my whole world had crashed and that there was nothing more to live for. I remember leaving my rooms and walking blindly out into the country; I walked all day and somewhere about nightfall I reached Swindon. I suppose I looked pretty wild, and I had no money and of course no luggage – anyhow, no one would give me a bed, so I tramped back again all through the night. I was all in when I got to Oxford, but I knew by then what I had to do. For Ruth's sake I had to carry on as though nothing had happened; I must disguise my feelings and go through all the polite motions of congratulation and good wishes and general rejoicing.

'I did it somehow – the hardest thing I'd ever done – and I even went further. Day by day I forced myself to try to know and to like Shirley; I wanted to see in him someone who was worthy of Ruth's love and who would make her happy. There again, in a sort of way, I succeeded. That was how I came to know Mary. I'd hardly noticed her before, because I'd had eyes for no one but Ruth, but gradually I came to think more and more of her. Winn, you must understand all this, or no one ever will. I've read somewhere that no man can ever really love two women in his life, but that's not true. I believe I loved Ruth as truly as any man can love a woman, yet I came to love Mary no less. I can't properly analyse my state of mind at that time. Bertrand Russell says somewhere that common

150

dislike of a third party is one of the great instinctive causes of mutual liking, but I believe there's a stronger motive than that. For Ruth's sake both Mary and I had made up our minds independently to like Shirley. We were always defending him against criticism, excusing his faults, softening down his asperities, concealing his angularities. Both of us were determined that Ruth should be happy in her married life, and because I wanted to do all that I could to help I forced myself to go not less but more often than ever before to the President's Lodgings. It was torture to me at first, but not for very long. So, you see, Mary and I fell into a kind of tacit alliance – an alliance to protect Ruth and Shirley from a censorious world – and gradually what had been a conscious deception became, for both of us, I believe, the simple truth. We saw that for all his bitterness and cynicism Shirley was indeed a good man at heart, a man with whom Ruth might be happy, and we struggled to make the world think so too. That was how Mary and I came together, and gradually, more and more, she herself filled my mind, until one day I came to the knowledge that I loved her, and that life might still hold for me a happiness which I had supposed lost for ever.

'Pride made me dissemble, and in my blindness I saw no danger in delay. It became an *idée fixe* with me that I would never go to her as a penniless and obscure scholar; I would wait until my work had brought me fame and a position in the world of learning. How different everything would be if I could speak to her as a man who had already made his mark, whose future was assured, who had some claim to hold up his head wherever he might be! I could not bear to think that she should ever be ashamed of me. So I worked with a new incentive and redoubled zeal, and I came very near to a great scientific triumph. Miserable, pathetic pride! I see my mistake all too clearly now. I fancy that she guessed my love, I believe that she was ready to reciprocate it. But as time passed and I made no sign I think she convinced herself that she had been wrong, and that I cared less for her than for my wretched research. She had her pride, too. You know the outcome. If Wimpfheimer had never followed out that particular line of inquiry at Freiburg I might now have my European reputation, but what does that matter? It's paltry, anyhow. It was Mary's engagement to Hargreaves last October that broke me, and destroyed my life.

'I can't talk of him with reason or restraint. To me from the first day I met him he represented every quality that I most dislike. It wasn't only that he was supercilious in a well-bred kind of way and that he was obviously contemptuous towards me and my work. No one likes that kind of attitude; it rankles when more important things are forgotten. But there was something more. He hadn't an ideal in him – he was just the materialist and the sensualist through and through. When I think of selfishness and egotism it is Hargreaves who springs at once to my mind. I don't believe that he ever gave one hour's thought to the good or well-being of anyone except himself. I know that he was popular and brilliant and successful, but who were his real friends? Weren't they all the self-satisfied, prosperous, successful people? Have you ever known him stretch out a hand to anyone who belonged to other classes of persons than those? How I hate what men call success! Just because he had been a good scholar and a notable athlete, and because he was well-off and well-connected, you all fell for him. You all thought of him as the finest product of Oxford and St Thomas's. Perhaps I'm unjust, but you know that he dominated you all. And yet he hasn't an ounce of pity or humanity or sympathy in his composition. Would he have sacrificed a single day's pleasure to help any one of us? Did he even think of any of the women in his life as anything more than a satisfaction to his desires or a plaything for his vanity? You know those buildings with a great pretentious façade and behind only a few mean shallow rooms; that's how I think of Hargreaves.

'Not that I worried at the beginning. He could go his way and I could go mine. I cared nothing for him – nothing until last October, when he became engaged to Mary. Fool that I was not to have foreseen some such disaster! How could I have imagined that no competitor would rob me of my prize? Yet how could I have thought that she would be deceived by such a man as Hargreaves? And yet again, why not? For being what she was she would only see his better side; the brilliance, the dominating masculinity. He had always the power to charm women when he wished.

'I've come to the hardest part of my tale, and again I beg you to try to understand. When that second blow fell my dislike of Hargreaves turned to a blazing hatred. It was an obsession, filling my life and my thoughts and my whole being, blotting out everything else. I would go to sleep thinking of him, I would wake up hating him with a new intensity. I could do no work, I could read no book. If I'd had one friend in whom I could have confided it might have been different, for there's healing in confession, but there was no one. So I brooded alone and stoked the fires of hate. Pray God, Winn, that you never know what human hate can mean. Brendel's quite right. You must know the man you hate inside out. Never have I known a fellow-creature as I came to know Hargreaves. I felt an overmastering desire to explore and expose every hidden chamber in that dark and selfish mind. My every hour was filled with the thought of him, and every hour the determination in me grew stronger that somehow, by hook or by crook, I would prevent him from marrying Mary. Surely in some way I could make it impossible for such a man to marry her – and kill all her happiness with his selfishness. For every other evil quality is forgivable, as it seems to me, except only that one. There's no hope and no forgiveness for the purely selfish man.

'It was madness, I suppose, madness and hate combined. I plunged into his life like a private detective tracking down a crime, or like a surgeon opening up a body for a major operation. But I wanted to kill rather than to cure. And the deeper I delved the more I was confirmed in my estimate of his character. It's wonderful what you can learn about a man if you make up your mind to find out, and I gave up all my time to the task. Conversations with those who had travelled with him in vacations, hints here, suggestions there. I see now how history can be written, if the historian applies himself wholeheartedly to his task, as I did to mine. Slowly I filled in the picture. We all knew, or guessed, that Hargreaves didn't live exactly a cloistered life out of term – why should he? – but none of you, except myself, knew how much of his life was spent in sordid amorous intrigues and in the pursuit of casual pleasure. It's not a pretty picture, but then the selfish sensualist is never an agreeable sight, and Hargreaves was nothing if not promiscuous. And somehow the fact that he lived his life in compartments – that up here in term he was, to all seeming, a respectable and respected member of society – made it worse in my eyes. I thought of that façade again, with all its magnificence and display, but behind it I seemed to picture mean tenements and festering slums.

'Then I discovered something else. Men that live the life that Hargreaves lived are apt to run risks, and he had not escaped. I needn't tell you in detail how I found that out. You know that I do blood-tests for Lorimer, and Hargreaves happened to be Lorimer's patient. Of course I oughtn't to have known whose tests I was making – but no one is always discreet, and even medical men among themselves sometimes let out secrets. I don't excuse myself for a moment; I had a suspicion and I ferreted out that secret. That's all there is to say about it. It was mean of me, no doubt, but I would have wormed knowledge of Hargreaves from the Sphinx herself if it had been necessary. Anyhow, I did find out, no matter exactly how. I'm not prudish – hardly any medical man is or can be. We think of disease of that kind rather as a stroke of ill-fortune than as a punishment for wrongdoing. Don't think for a moment that I set up as a moralist, or as a judge of my fellow-men. But there was something in this particular case which gave me a feeling of loathing and repulsion, and fanned my hatred to a more savage blaze. I mustn't be technical, but it was just this. When Hargreaves became engaged in October I was still getting positive reaction from his blood-tests; in other words, he had no right to ask any woman then to share his life. A decent man must have waited, must have postponed that step until he had the certainty of a cure. For a cure can be certain and generally is. But you can't fathom the selfishness of a man like Hargreaves.

'Wasn't it natural that I should bend all my energies to prevent that cursed marriage? Wasn't I justified a hundred times over in trying to do so? Day by day the conviction became stronger that, by fair means or foul, I would stop him from ruining Mary's life. But how could I do it? There's too much of the Hamlet in every one of us; I thought and schemed and brooded, but I couldn't screw up my courage to act. Time and again I rehearsed all that I might – that I must – say, and time after time I could not bring myself to the scratch. I saw in anticipation all too vividly how he would receive me. He would sneer at my interference and bludgeon down my arguments. How could I, who had always failed, hope to find words to move Hargreaves, who had always dominated, always succeeded, always had his own way? I felt the miserable burden of my own weakness –

I loathed my own incompetence and powerlessness. So for weeks I hesitated, torn between timidity and overwhelming hatred.

'Last week I knew that I could not delay much longer. Come what might, I must put it to the touch, or I should go mad under a strain which never eased. On that fatal Wednesday evening I had at last come to a decision; I came down to Hall with the fixed intention of speaking to Hargreaves that night. Some time later I would go to his rooms; I would tell him how much I knew of his manner of life; I would threaten, whatever the consequences, to spread abroad the scandals of his private affairs unless he would take steps to terminate his engagement. And if he refused to listen to me, if he threw me out of his rooms, as I half anticipated that he would, I would translate my threat into action, come what might.

'You remember the conversation at dinner that night, and all that Brendel said? Of course you do. Anyone would have been interested, but for me his words had a special and a personal significance. When he spoke of the psychology of the murderer I realized the extent of my own hatred of Hargreaves; when he described the murderer watching and studying his victim I realized how I had watched and studied my own enemy. Yet, as I sat in Common Room, there was no thought of murder in my mind. I swear to you that then, at least, I had no thought of that. When I left you at nine o'clock my intentions were clear and innocent enough. I would go to my Lab. and think out again for the thousandth time just what words I should use to Hargreaves. I could not sit quietly waiting in Common Room – I had to get away somewhere where I could be alone until the time came to speak.

'It was here in my Lab. – here where you will find my body, and where perhaps you will read all this – that I became a murderer in my heart. On my table was lying

156

Wimpfheimer's account of his discovery, the discovery which might have been mine. I glanced at it again, and I realized how the merest chance had robbed me of reputation, and now the work of four years and more that I had done in that very room was utterly wasted. I had failed, and I should always fail. Twice I had seen the hope of a lifelong happiness, and twice I had missed my opportunity; once fame had been within my reach, and I had been too slow to grasp it. Was it not certain that I should fail again in my mission to Hargreaves that night? What use was I to the world, or ever would be? And then suddenly, blindingly, the thought of murder filled my mind. I saw the loaded revolver lying on the octagonal table as Hargreaves had described it; I saw the destined victim sitting in his chair. One sudden irrevocable act would destroy the whole edifice of doubt and difficulty. The death of Hargreaves would solve every problem. Mary would grieve for a while, but time heals and her life was still before her. Of myself I thought little. I had nothing to live for, and for a man in my position and with my knowledge suicide would be easy. I need only wait a few days, and quietly give myself the fatal dose. A mental breakdown, a moment of madness, over-work, over-strain – how easy it would be to explain, how easy to excuse! No one would be the poorer by my going.

'My brain, when once the decision was made, worked with amazing clearness. There were three possibilities and I considered them all. Hargreaves might not yet have returned to his rooms. In that case the oak would still be sported, and I must go away till a later hour. Or again he might be in his rooms, but not alone. If that was so I should hear voices inside when I reached the outer room, and I could depart unobserved to wait a better opportunity. The third possibility was the one for which I hoped, and on which indeed I counted. The oak would be open, the lights would be on, and Hargreaves would be sitting alone in his rooms.'

My throat was growing tired, and for a moment I paused in my reading. Brendel spoke for the first time.

'Prendergast argued very clearly, but he never noticed that Mottram had left the Common Room before Shirley went up to Hargreaves' rooms – and yet everything turns on that. Go on, if you will.'

# CHAPTER SIXTEEN

I took up the manuscript again, and continued to read it aloud.

'If he was alone, what then? I visualized quite clearly what would happen. He would be sitting reading or working, either at his writing-table or in his arm-chair by its side. I would fling open the door, pick up the revolver off the table, take a couple of paces forward and shoot him as he sat there, without a second's pause or hesitation. No one would notice a shot on an evening when undergraduates were letting off fireworks and firing revolvers in the Quad. Two minutes after I had shot him I should be sitting in my own room ... It only takes five minutes in the car from my Lab. to the college, but during that drive I killed Hargreaves a hundred times. I went through every detail in my plan until I could have done it all blindfold, and not one thought of pity or remorse crossed my mind. When I'd parked the car outside I took a bunch of keys from my pocket to open the Fellows' door. I noticed then that I'd put on a pair of gloves in the car without thinking what I was doing. They were an old pair of wash-leather gloves which I always keep in the car, for it's cold going up and down to the Lab. at night-time. I was just putting them into my pocket when I thought of fingerprints and pulled them on again. If I hadn't thought of them then I suppose there would have been enough evidence to hang me. Somehow the fact that I'd so nearly made a fatal slip gave me new confidence; I felt that nothing else could go wrong, that some outside agency was guiding me. I felt cool and determined and certain of my prey. Yes – that was my state of mind. All doubts and inhibitions had left me; I was the beast of prey crouching before its kill.

'Very quietly I walked up Hargreaves' stairs. His oak

was open, so I knew that he was in. There was no sound, so I knew that he was alone. In the outer room I paused for a moment to gather myself together. I remember thinking – how oddly the mind works! – that Hargreaves had loved in Common Room to lay down the law about the theory of games to a sycophantic audience. "Keep your eye on the ball is the secret of all games. Brain and eyes and muscles will work in perfect harmony if you observe that simple principle." What rubbish such talk had always seemed to me, but now I reflected with grim humour that I would follow the advice of my own victim. I must think of nothing and look at nothing except the revolver in the half-second after my entry. Once it was in my hand I must take two paces forward for the shot which could not miss.

'I grasped the handle and pushed open the door; I seized the revolver and stepped two paces forward. As I shot him he was sitting in the large leather arm-chair next to the writing-table. Over the back of it only his head was visible, and of that only the outline, for he was reading by the aid of a reading-lamp on the writing-table, and all the other lights were out. He half turned his head as I stepped forward – there was no time for more.'

*

For the second time Brendel's voice interrupted me, but this time he seemed to be talking to himself.

'Yes, it is quite true; I have made that experiment to see. If you put a reading-lamp on the far side of a man in an arm-chair you will see only the bare outline of his head; he sits in his own light. And Mottram was a myope, too. But Cotter made his one mistake there. He never considered that the other lights might have been turned on *after* the murder. Go on, if you are ready.'

Again I took up Mottram's manuscript.

*

'At the very moment that I pulled the trigger I knew that there was some hideous mistake, and as the body sagged in the chair I saw that it was not Hargreaves but Shirley who lay dead before me. No words, Winn, can describe to you what I felt then. If all the tortures of the damned were concentrated for you into one short minute you could not suffer more than I suffered then. I sprang to him, tore off my gloves, and undid his shirt to feel his heart, but I knew that he was dead before ever my hand touched him. Then I sat down on a chair and thought what I should do.

'It was the reading-lamp that had betrayed me. You can't see a man's features when he's between you and it, when there's no other light. Besides I'm short-sighted at the best of times. Remember I'd done it all in far less time that it takes to tell. Go to that room; stand beside that table; put the arm-chair where it stood that Wednesday night; place the reading-lamp on the corner of the writing-table – and you will see that his head was in a straight line – a dead straight line – between me and the lamp. I swear to God that it happened like that. Murder was in my heart, but I would have harmed no human creature except Hargreaves. Yet think what I had done! I had shot almost my only friend; I had left Ruth a widow; I had made Mary's unhappy marriage even more certain than before.

'My first instinct was to drive straight back to the Lab. and end it all then and there, but gradually as I sat gazing at that dead body another plan formed in my mind. No one, apparently, had heard the fatal shot. In the far Quad I heard the sound of distant revellers, like an echo from a different world. Why should I not go as I had come, and leave the crime a mystery? And then in some way or other I would still bring about what I most desired; somehow I would still stop Hargreaves from marrying Mary. Then, and only then, I could put an end to my wretched life with the assurance that I had done at least one good deed to set in my account against this hideous crime. I put on my gloves again; I turned on all the lights to make sure that I had left no traces; I put the revolver back in its place on the octagonal table; I walked down the stairs and out of the college; I drove back to the Lab.

'What happened next is hard even for me to understand. I sat down and began to work. You'll hardly credit that, but it's true nevertheless. I had to steady my mind, and I turned instinctively to what I had always done. I suppose it was sheer force of habit. A few minutes afterwards Holt of Magdalen, who works in the same building, came in to see me. What he said I've not the faintest idea, but I imagine that he noticed nothing out of the ordinary. After he left I sat here until midnight, and then I drove back to college. I went to bed, and went to sleep. Yes, for eight hours I slept like a tired child – as though I'd never slept before. But I've never slept properly for an hour since then.

'You won't want me to describe the next few days to you; it doesn't need much imagination to fill in the gaps there. Everything happened as I had expected, for my alibi was no worse than that of all the rest. Only I felt that Brendel guessed my secret, and sometimes I thought that Cotter did too. I made up my mind that I'd tackle Hargreaves after the funeral. If I failed then I must abandon hope.

'Winn, you surprised us at the end of that interview; so you can guess how he took it. If ever I saw a man's naked soul I saw it then. I told him what he was – somehow the words came and I didn't spare him – and I told him that I'd bare his character to the world if he dared to marry Mary. Could he face it if all his acquaintances knew of his phil-anderings and of his disease? I gave him two days to break that engagement – two days and not an hour more. And when I finished he just crumpled – pitifully, miserably! He began with bluster, and he ended in collapse. How wretched these strong men are when they break down! He was selfish enough to sacrifice Mary to himself, but he wouldn't face publicity or criticism. He surrendered without conditions, but he blurted out one paltry request: Couldn't it all be kept secret for a time at least? He would break the engagement at once if I would pledge myself to silence, but no one need know what had been done. Later he would get permission from the college to take a term's leave of absence, and the public announcement could be made then. I agreed to that. It didn't matter to me whether the rest of the world knew or not. I stipulated only that I should know from Mary herself that the engagement was broken. As we talked I knew what I had guessed before – I knew that he never really loved her. He wanted a wife to make a comfortable home for him; he wanted someone who would be a credit to him and to his house; he thought that when Vereker's days as President ended he would stand more chance to succeed him as a married man – and particularly as a man who had married Mary Vereker. I could read him like an open book. I said before that I saw his naked soul – I saw it again in every bare and mean and selfish detail. When you left me that night, Winn, I laughed, yes, laughed like a fiend in Hell. For I know now that if I'd gone to him at the beginning and said my say he'd have given in just as he gave in then. And I'd killed Shirley and condemned myself to death because I'd been afraid to tackle him. He's a rotten man and bogus and a coward, but I'd been a coward too.

'I believe that he went to see Mary that same evening, but he'd reckoned without her spirit. I can't tell what passed, but I can guess. When she saw him as he really was she must have swept all his mean excuses and prevarications aside. It wasn't in her to act a lie to save his face and avoid comment, and so *she* sent that notice to *The Times* that you read this morning.

'There's not much more to tell. Mary sent me a little

stiff formal note on Tuesday – her engagement had been broken off and she was going away for a few days; she thought that I might like to know this for I had always been a friend; there would be an announcement in the papers shortly. I knew that I had won then, but I waited to read the announcement, and when I saw it I knew a moment's happiness again. But I knew too that my part was played out and that I must go. I was still looking at *The Times* this morning when Brendel came in, and asked me to drive with him over the Downs. I don't know quite why I agreed, except that one can't refuse him when he's in earnest. We got out of the car somewhere near Wootton Bassett and then we walked over the downland. He'll tell you what we said to one another. Somehow I'd always felt that he guessed from the beginning.

*

'A man like myself hasn't any affairs to set in order. I've no one dependent on me and no friends. That makes it all easy. And I know I'm right. How could I go on living, knowing all the time that I was a murderer? I couldn't face it. Brendel knows what I mean to do, I'm sure of that, though I've not told him. I've asked him to bring you up to-night, and he must know what I mean by that. He thinks I'm right, too, though he wouldn't say so. One sees pretty clearly when one's waiting for the end.

'That's the whole story. Someone had to hear it, and you've always tried to be kind to me, though I don't think you ever saw very deep. Besides, there's one thing I want you to do. You must make quite sure that Mary is saved from any unnecessary grief or scandal. There's another letter here, which I've written for the rest of them all to read. It's the letter I ought to have written if I'd been the ordinary suicide. A nervous breakdown due to the failure of my research and the shock of the death of my friend Shirley –

164

that is what they must all think. After all what could be more natural? Overwork and overstrain, disappointment and a temporary loss of mental balance. A brilliant young scientist cut off on the threshold of his career! My God, I could make the Coroner's speech myself! Above all, Winn, never let Mary know; she has enough to bear without that.'

*

The letter stopped as abruptly as it had begun. I looked up and observed that Brendel was wiping his glasses with meticulous care just as he had done on that fatal evening a week before. When he spoke his voice was curiously gentle.

'Yes, I knew that he meant to destroy himself, and I believe that he was right to do so. How could he go on living? It would have been a drawn-out torture, a daily death. But I was afraid that his nerve might fail him at the end. For he's right – there is too much of Hamlet in most of us, and though Mottram was a brave man in a way he was a weak man too. Twice perhaps he might have won happiness if he'd had the strength of will to grasp it, and twice he waited and did nothing. And then his work. Do you realize that if he'd stuck to that instead of allowing this hatred of Hargreaves to obsess him he, and not Wimpfheimer, would probably have been first with this discovery, and his name would be known now to every scientific man in Europe? No, fate forgives much, but it never forgives weakness. Read me that other letter.'

I opened the second envelope and read the contents aloud, but I cannot transcribe them. Mottram was a weakling, perhaps, but he had carried out his plan to the end. The latter was, as he had promised, the letter which he ought to have written – the letter of a nervous, hypersensitive man who had momentarily lost his mental equilibrium. To a coroner's jury it would appear pathetic enough, but to me who knew the truth it seemed a last superb gesture, a piece of the finest acting, infinitely tragic.

I replaced it in its envelope and laid it on the table. Brendel looked at his watch and got up.

'Come,' he said; 'there are things which we must do.'

# CHAPTER SEVENTEEN

BRENDEL'S words roused me to a sudden realization of our responsibilities.

'We've been here half an hour and we haven't called the police or done anything to get help. What can we have been thinking of? There must be a telephone outside; let's find it and call them up at once.'

I sprang to my feet in a fury of belated impatience, but Brendel motioned me back to my chair.

'No, not this time. It will be better if we go to fetch them. For us, at any rate, there is no mystery to solve, and nothing can be done for Mottram. But first put that document carefully in your pocket where it can't be seen, and the short letter back on the table where we found it. Thank you.'

He looked round the room carefully before we left it, and, from outside, locked the door. Then we stepped out into the night. Eleven o'clock was striking from all the clocks of Oxford as I got into the car and took the driver's seat. Brendel sat beside me in silence, but we had hardly gone a quarter of a mile when he suddenly told me to stop the car. Too much surprised to question him, I obeyed. He jumped briskly out, opened the bonnet in front, and for a few minutes so far as I could see busied himself with the engine. Then his head re-emerged from the bonnet.

'Now see if she will start.'

I tried and failed.

'What the devil have you been doing,' I exclaimed; 'are you mad?'

'Not at all, I've been making a little adjustment. Listen to me, and listen carefully. We can't afford to make any mistake of detail. It may not have occurred to you that, as I have often remarked, Inspector Cotter is a very competent man. He will certainly connect these two deaths with one another, and it may cross his mind to examine our movements to-night rather carefully and to check up the times. If he does that he will certainly notice that we spent about half an hour in Mottram's laboratory before we sent for the police. How are we going to explain that without telling the truth about Mottram's confession? We've got to gain half an hour somehow. Listen. This is what you must say if you are questioned about our movements.' He paused and thought carefully for a moment before he continued his instructions. 'We didn't look at the time but we left college somewhere after ten and before half past – probably about ten-twenty.'

'But it was certainly not later than ten past,' I objected.

Brendel made a gesture of annoyance at my obtuseness.

'Forget that, please. You will say that we left round about ten-twenty, so far as you remember. The car was cold and wouldn't start, and ran very badly on the way up. We must have reached the laboratory soon after ten-thirty. That's a quarter of an hour gained on the journey out. After discovering the body our first thought was to rush down for the police. We started and the car broke down here. For ten minutes we tried everything we could think of to start her up again, and we couldn't, so we hailed a passing car. Luckily they're few and far between on this road at this time of night. There's the other quarter of an hour accounted for. Have you got that all clearly in your mind?'

'But you want me to perjure myself, Brendel,' I protested.

'Of course I do. The important thing is that you should perjure yourself successfully. There mustn't be any bungling about this.'

'I can't do it. I'm no use at deception and I shall break down if I try it.'

'Rubbish. You can do it and you must. Can't you imagine what Miss Vereker's position will be if all the truth comes out? If Mottram was prepared to kill himself rather than let that happen you must be prepared to tell a few very white lies. Are you agreed?'

I nodded helplessly. What else could I do?

'Very well then. Now repeat the time-table of our movements to make sure that you have it all right.'

Obediently I did so, and Brendel signified his approval.

'Good. Ah ...'

At the end of the stretch he had observed the lights of an oncoming car, and running into the middle of the road he began wildly moving his arms and shouting. The car stopped with a jerk, just in time to prevent a further catastrophe, and a surprised and angry-looking face was thrust out of the window. It was then that I realized what a magnificent actor Brendel would have made. The calm, the lawyer-like precision, the air of command with which he had addressed me were all gone. In a moment he had become an excited and breathless person, who had lost his head in an emergency, and he poured out a flood of words upon the stranger.

'There's been an awful accident. For Heaven's sake take us to the police station. A terrible tragedy. A man's killed himself, and our car's broken down. Get us to the police station as quickly as ever you can. He's killed himself and we must get help from the police ...'

'What's it all about?' said the stranger. 'Has there been a car crash, and who's hurt, anyhow?'

'No, no,' I interposed, 'a man has committed suicide in his laboratory – at least we think so, and we were going to the police station to get help when our car broke down. Can you run us down there?'

'Righto. Jump in. The station's just by the Town Hall, isn't it?'

Five minutes later we were standing before the sergeant on duty in the police station.

There, and during our drive back to the laboratory, Brendel poured out his story once more, and I corroborated the details. Yes, he had become very friendly with Mottram during his stay in Oxford. He was interested in his work too, and had often visited him in his laboratory to talk about it, and to see how he was getting on. He had been worried a good deal by Mottram's bad state of health and particularly by his obvious mental depression during the last few days. (The Herr Inspektor would remember that there had been a mysterious murder at the dead man's college, which had doubtless preyed on his mind.) That very morning he had persuaded Mottram to take a long drive with him out into the country in the hope that he might cheer him up, and he had seemed, certainly, happier when they came back. But he, Brendel, was still anxious about his friend, and had arranged to go up in the evening to the laboratory to fetch him home when he had finished his work, because he thought that Mottram should not be left too long alone. It was a fine night and Mr Winn ('who is sitting by you') had offered to accompany him. Yes, they had left college about twenty minutes past ten. Then, followed the tale, as he had taught it to me. I winced as the sergeant jotted down the false times and details, but I corroborated each of them in turn.

'We reached the laboratory about half past ten,' Brendel was saying. 'I had the keys because Mottram had given them to me that afternoon, in case he didn't hear me from his room when I arrived, so we walked straight in, Mr Winn and I. We found his body in his chair, and a letter lying on the table, saying that he couldn't bear it all, and that he had committed suicide. I'm afraid that the terrible shock made us lose our heads rather; we ought to have found the telephone and called you up, but we were so upset and horrified that our first thought was to run to the car and drive down to the police station for help. You see I am a foreigner and don't know about things in this country, and Mr Winn' (his voice sank to a whisper which I imagine I was not supposed to hear) . . . 'was an old friend and colleague and temporarily quite unfit to think of what should be done. Yes, I did remember to lock up the room before we left. Then the car broke down on the way to the police station, and we couldn't make it start again, so we had to hail the first car that passed. You know the rest.'

The car stopped. We entered the building, and once more we stood in that room of death.

\*

It was long past midnight when at last we returned to my rooms, but sleep was impossible, and I implored Brendel to stay with me for a time.

'At least,' I said, 'tell me how you discovered all this.'

'All right,' he replied, 'but first oblige me by locking up that letter in a place where no one save yourself can find it. That at least we owe to Mottram.'

I obeyed, and we settled down once more into the arm-chairs from which we had so often before discussed the problem of the murder.

'When did you first know that Mottram had done it?' I asked.

'This morning, to be exact, just before noon, when he told me so. But that's starting at the end. If you had asked me when I first *guessed* who it was the answer could have been equally precise. I should have said at about twenty-five minutes past ten on the night of the murder, when you and I and Hargreaves stood looking at Shirley's body. Yes, I guessed then . . . but let me explain.

'The moment that Hargreaves came back and told us what he had found in his rooms one thought flashed through my mind; it was exactly that thought which Prendergast put before us the next evening. Who knew that Shirley was in the Dean's rooms, and who knew too that a loaded revolver was lying on the table? The answer was instantaneous. Of course there was no certainty, but I knew that it was overwhelmingly probable that murder had been committed by one of those who had dined with us that night. Immediately, therefore, I bent all my energies to fixing in my mind the picture of those diners, of their expressions, their behaviour, and their words. I tried to photograph them in my mind before the impression had time to fade. Of course I was a stranger and, with a party of thirteen, some of the impressions were inevitably dim, but I am an observant man, and of most, indeed of nearly all, of those thirteen, I had a clear mental picture. In the minute or so that elapsed while we ran to Hargreaves' room (and you ran faster than I did!) I had already passed them under review, and I was sorting them out even while I was looking at the body.

'It's a way of mine to think of men in terms of natural objects. Sometimes I see them as trees or shrubs or flowers, sometimes as hills and mountains, but most often of all as streams and rivers. Often in the course of my work at home I have to travel from Vienna to Prague, and from Prague to Dresden and Berlin. Have you ever travelled that way? You should, for it's grand country. *Ein selten gesegnetes Land.* At Prague I've watched the Moldau a hundred times; it's a fine stream, broad and beautiful, and spanned by one bridge at least that'll bear comparison with any. Yes, a fine and worthy stream, and impressive, too, in its way. And then further on in my journey, half-way to Dresden, perhaps, I've looked out from the carriage window and seen the Elbe. At first sight, in some places, it isn't much to look at; as it runs down the gorge between the hills it seems narrow and smooth and not very big – but wait! I notice a great powerful steamer, tugging and straining against the stream, with the waters, elsewhere seemingly quiet, surging at its bows. Then I know that beneath the Elbe is a mighty river, full of hidden power and energy, and I recollect that it carries in it its own waters and all those of my poor Moldau as well. A mighty river, strong and secret! And perhaps next day I am in Berlin, looking at the poor little Spree, all banked and controlled and conventionalized. Don't think me an imaginative idiot; men's minds, you know, all work in different ways.

'Well, I thought of those thirteen diners just like that. How many had left on my mind the impression of power beneath the surface! Shirley, certainly, but he was dead; Prendergast, for that clear intellectualism often masks a drama of feelings and desires; Mottram, for I had marked the play of emotion on his face whilst he sat so strangely silent at dinner; Hargreaves without doubt and perhaps one or other of the scientists, but I couldn't tell. But the rest? Doyne, for example. He may be a great man some day, for he has character, but it's not fully developed. For me he's "the stripling Thames at Bablockhythe" – a great river later on but not yet. And Mitton – he was just a pleasant babbling brook. And Trower? – well I can't quite describe him; he was like a river on the films, great waterfalls and acres of water, but really all an elaborate pretence – not a real river at all. Of them all, Mottram and Hargreaves were the most incalculable, full of rapids and whirlpools and hidden sunken rocks. So it was on these two chiefly that my thoughts centred as we climbed the stairs. Remember that repressions and inhibition are the forerunners of excesses.

'When we entered the room and looked at the body, I said to myself, "Mottram," and I said it for one reason and one alone. Shirley's shirt was open at the front. If *you* killed a man in cold blood your first instinct would be to get away from the body. A kind of repulsion, a sort of fear, perhaps, would come over you. I don't think you would touch the body if you could possibly avoid it. But Mottram had had a medical training, and with him habit would be too strong. His first and overpowering instinct would be to assure himself that the victim was dead. He would feel his heart – he could not do otherwise. Already that night then I had guessed the truth; Mottram had shot Shirley, though of his reasons I had no inkling.

'On Thursday night at dinner I watched him with absorbed interest, and the conviction grew upon me with irresistible force that though he might be, and probably was, a murderer, he was most certainly not a criminal by nature. That was why I tried to keep out of the investigation, and why I told you that I was afraid of what I should find. You compelled me to explore the mystery, and I couldn't refuse.

'Of course I was still in the realm of guesswork, and I had to be sure that I was not making some ghastly mistake. On one pretext or another I began to interview everyone who had been present that night, in order to confirm or adjust my first impressions of them. Those interviews didn't change my mind at all, but I soon saw that, if my theory was correct, it was of primary importance to know, if possible, exactly who was in possession of all the relevant facts before the murder took place. That was the reason why I made my map of the college and staged that little game on Saturday night. It was a very useful piece of reconstruction, too, and your recollection of the course of events was invaluable. For one fact of immense significance emerged, and it was this, Mottram had gone out of Common Room *before* Shirley announced that he was going up to Hargreaves' rooms. That fact, once I had established it, gave me something new to work on, and I made certain deductions from it. Of course it was possible to take the view that it cleared Mottram of suspicion; he could not suppose that Shirley would be there, and therefore he would never have gone there to shoot him. That, I must admit, was my own first reaction. Yet, as I considered all the other possibilities, I remained convinced that Mottram was still the most likely murderer. I couldn't get that open shirt out of my mind. And so gradually I came to the true answer – supposing that Mottram had intended to shoot Hargreaves, and had shot Shirley by mistake? That was surely very unlikely, but it was not impossible. Mottram was a myope, as I had observed, and he would probably have been in a state of nervous excitement when the tragedy occurred. As to the lights – well there I do give myself some credit for an imaginative reconstruction – it *did* occur to me, though Cotter missed the point, that though all the lights were on when Hargreaves found the body, they might have been turned on by the murderer after the crime was committed.

'Granted the truth of my assumption the whole nature of the problem had altered. I had to find a motive for Mottram's intention to shoot Hargreaves, whereas before I had been trying to find out why he should have shot Shirley. The obvious answer seemed to be sexual jealousy. That's a powerful incentive to crime, and it seemed to be the only explanation which was at all likely to fit the facts. You see why I wanted to interview Miss Vereker, and why I had to do so on the pretext of talking to her sister.' Brendel paused and shifted uneasily in his chair. 'And, I must confess it to you, that wasn't my only reason for wanting to interview Miss Vereker. I may as well make a clean breast of it now, though I took some care to keep you in the dark about it at the time. The truth is that I had an uneasy suspicion of *her* all the time at the back of my mind.'

'Of Mary Vereker?' I exclaimed in amazement.

'Yes. Don't think too hardly of me; I'd not met her then. I couldn't help feeling that my original theory *might* be all wrong, and if it was, then suspicion must turn on her. That door into the President's Lodgings fascinated me. She herself fulfilled, too, so many of the necessary conditions.

Shirley was her brother-in-law, and she must have known him very intimately; there might well have been family quarrels of long standing, or hidden tales of jealousy and hate. Besides how easily she could have done it! I could picture her slipping out from her father's house to pay a brief visit to her fiancé; finding her brother-in-law there instead of him – and the revolver on the table. And all the details presented no insuperable difficulty; ladies are more likely to carry gloves than men, and Shirley, who would naturally jump up from his chair if a stranger entered, might well have remained seated when his sister-in-law came in. Besides I know well that there are many women with nerves of steel, and determination which nothing will shake. She must often have walked across to Hargreaves' room; who was likely to suspect her? And she would have been back in her father's house long before her absence would be noticed. Well, I went to see her, and, thank God, I came away from that rather uncomfortable interview with an impression that amounted almost to certainty that Miss Vereker, even if she was the innocent cause of a deadly rivalry between two men, knew nothing about the matter whatever, and had no suspicion of the truth. Don't let us speak of that ugly thought of mine. After I had seen her and spoken to her I put it from my mind and I felt doubly certain that my original theory must be the true one.

'As you know, then, I eliminated all the other possibilities except Hargreaves and Mottram, and more and more I became convinced that suspicion rested far more heavily on the latter. But it was still all a matter of guesswork and surmise, and beyond that I couldn't get. Cotter was perfectly right; there were no clues to follow up at all, and I began to despair of getting any confirmation of my theory.

'It was in that state of mind that I went to the funeral. A funeral is an emotional business, and I thought it not unlikely that I should see a little further into Mottram's heart, though I'll not pretend that I enjoyed doing detection work in circumstances like those.'

Brendel paused for a moment, as though he wished to rid himself of an unpleasant memory. Then he continued.

'We've some great descriptive writers in Germany, Winn, but I dare say you've not read many of them. One day I'll lend you a story by Stefan Zweig; called *Vierundzwanzig Stunden aus dem Leben einer Frau*. It's a grand piece of writing. It's the story of a woman married to a wealthy husband, who used to gamble at Monte Carlo. She was bored by the gambling, but she used to watch the gamblers, and after a time she saw that it was more exciting to watch their hands than their faces. Her husband died, but she still haunted the rooms, because it filled her time and gave her interest. And always she watched the hands, and read in them every emotion of hope and triumph, of terror and despair. One day she saw a pair of hands, more expressive than any she had seen before – at one moment they were poised like an animal waiting for its spring, the next they advanced with tigerish cupidity to seize the spoil, and then a little later they would sink back into a kind of feline repose, ready to turn in an instant to action. She watched them, fascinated by their beauty and muscular power and cruelty and intensity of purpose. And then at the end, suddenly, they dropped on the table as though all life and hope had left them, and she knew, knew with a horrible certainty, that the end had come, and that the owner of those hands had decided that death was preferable to a hopeless struggle. The rest of the tale doesn't matter – you shall read it for yourself; but think now, as I often do, of the hands and all that they betray. I have been told by some lawyers that they listen for the feet – that the witness may control his features and clutch the edge of the witness-box with his hands, but that his feet shuffle and rattle on the floor as he tells a lie. It may be so – I don't know – but the hands are usually good enough for me. You will remember that I went to the funeral, and you may even have noticed that I took pains to sit almost behind Mottram in the chapel. There I watched his hands, and they were the hands of a tortured man! There was further confirmation at the cemetery. I wonder if you observed that at one moment Miss Vereker looked like fainting? I did, and so did Mottram. His eyes had never left her as we stood near the grave, and he moved in an instant to support her, but Hargreaves, who was next to her, and who was engaged to her – Hargreaves never noticed. I don't think he gave a thought to her all through.

'When I got back from the funeral I felt sure that I was right, but still I had no proof, and I began to wonder what I should do next. It was then that you came to see me and told me of the talk which you had interrupted between Mottram and Hargreaves, and of the extraordinary request of Mottram that you should hold your hand for three days at least. Exactly what he meant I could not tell, but I could hazard a fairly shrewd guess. There must be some sort of an arrangement between the two, and there must be some sort of a *dénouement* to be expected soon. Whatever was in store for us I could see no possible harm in waiting, and so I advised you to do as Mottram asked.

'I did nothing more until I read that announcement in *The Times*, and then I knew that the drama had reached its climax. For a brief moment I was inclined to revise my whole theory. Did it not seem that Hargreaves had been the murderer, that Mottram knew it, and that he had used his knowledge to force Hargreaves to break his engagement? It was even possible that Mottram had surprised the other red-handed; that would explain the open shirt. Somehow my instinct made me reject that explanation, though logically I could not ignore the possibility of its being true. I still clung to my former theory, though I had to adapt it to the new fact. Clearly, if Mottram was guilty, he had some hold over Hargreaves, some power which was sufficient to make the latter obey him. I could not know all the details, but I was, all things considered, surprisingly near the truth. The new danger I also foresaw. Even if Mottram was a murderer he had neither the temperament nor the insensibility to live on under the shadow of an undiscovered crime. If, as I now guessed, he had been waiting for this engagement to be terminated, was it not only too likely that he would cut all the knots by an act of self-destruction? I could not, of course, understand all his motives, but the danger of suicide was apparent to me. I went straight to him, and begged him to come for a long drive with me into the country. His surprise was evident but I simply wouldn't let him refuse. I had another reason too. He had come from the north, from a country of hills and moors; I wanted to get him out on to the Downs, for I knew he'd talk more freely out there. Some men are choked down in the valleys. We drove out through Wantage and Hungerford to Marlborough and on to Wootton Bassett, and then we left the car and walked on. He had the sort of simplicity of a man who has lived much to himself, even though at times he tried to dramatize himself a little (you noticed that in his letter?) but then weak men are always apt to be a little melodramatic. He talked of his early life, and of his struggles, and of his work. And then at last, when we'd walked a long way we began to speak of Shirley's death, and he asked me whom I thought to be the murderer. I think I'd always known all through that walk that he would ask some such question, and I had my answer ready. Very carefully and very quietly I gave him my reconstruction of the crime, and when I'd finished I asked him whether that was what had happened and he said "Yes." Then he filled in a few of the missing details – about the gloves and the reading-lamp and all that, as though he were telling a story about someone we'd both known years ago. When he finished he said,

179

"I think we ought to get back to Oxford now; I want to write it all down to-day," and so we went back to the car. We talked about the country and the hills, and a host of things like that, but never another word about the crime. But on the way back he asked me if I'd mind coming up in the evening about ten to fetch him from the Lab. I said that of course I would, and he asked if I'd bring you with me. Then I knew what he meant to do. I said nothing to stop him; it would have been useless, and I think it would have been wrong.'

Brendel paused reflectively, and watched the smoke from his cigar drifting upwards. Then he spoke again with a sudden fierceness.

'I'm not afraid of that responsibility. I should do the same again. He couldn't have lived with all that burden to bear.'

His voice sank to its customary calmer tone.

'You see, Winn, I didn't perform any great feat of detection. I only applied a few very simple principles. I told you that first evening, and I repeat it now, that in any given case the number of possible murderers is ridiculously small, and in this special case circumstances reduced the number still more. Only one of those who dined could have done it, and of them nearly all were ruled out for general or special reasons. And yet, for all that, viewed simply as a crime Shirley's murder had some aspects which made it extraordinarily interesting. It was, you see, to begin with, almost a perfect murder. The opportunity was there, so that the murderer need leave no clue of any kind whatever. And it had one really remarkable feature. No single person connected with it told a lie – except Callendar, and he confessed to you almost as soon as he had told it. Even Mottram told the strict truth to Prendergast, when he was asked to describe his movements that night. He left out a good deal, but he told no lie. I wonder what he would have said if Prendergast had asked each suspect in turn whether he had killed Shirley. I'm not at all sure he wouldn't have confessed. Still, that's all hypothetical. The fact remains that no protagonist told a lie. Yet in almost all crimes the culprit is discovered because he had lied. He tells one lie to cover his tracks, and that one lie is the parent of others – till at last the whole fabric crashes. Consider the case of the man who tries to manufacture a false alibi, or the case of the man who uses poison. There is always one lie necessary in the beginning, and that invariably has to be bolstered up with others, till the whole mechanism of the culprit's everyday life breaks down. I daresay I'm mixing my metaphors, but you'll see what I mean. But in this case there was no lie, and that is precisely why a really competent man like Cotter could never get going. He couldn't find a clue, and he couldn't find a false statement which might have started him off. Yet you noticed how quickly he was on the trail of Callendar's little suppression of the truth and your collusion. Well, I think that's about all, and it's probably enough to destroy your belief in me as a detective; you see, I did nothing but put two and two together and make the answer four. But perhaps there are questions you'd like to ask about it?'

'No, no,' I said, 'I don't depreciate what you did at all. It's wonderful to me that a stranger could have noticed so much, and argued so clearly. But there are two questions I want to ask you.'

'Go ahead, then.'

'The first is this. Would Cotter have discovered that Mottram was the murderer if you'd not been here?'

'I think Cotter has a very shrewd idea now. I've always said that he was, within his limits, a very competent man, and I'm pretty certain that he eliminated everyone save Mottram and Hargreaves, just as I did. He works slowly, but surely. Of the two he would certainly suspect Mottram, for he's a type that Cotter can't really understand. Hargreaves is the sort of man with whom he is accustomed to deal, and whom he appreciates. But he was up against a brick wall, for he couldn't find any motive for the murder. You'd be surprised if I told you how often Cotter had been up to Mottram's laboratory to see him on some pretext or other. Yes, I'm sure he suspected Mottram, but he couldn't prove anything. If Mottram had brazened it out and kept his mouth shut no one on earth could ever have proved that he was guilty. Now that he's dead Cotter will feel sure that he was the murderer, but still he can prove nothing whatever, and his lips will be sealed. What was the other question?'

'Just this. Why on earth did Hargreaves wait ten minutes before he went up to his rooms after he had left Common Room?'

Something like the old smile flickered round Brendel's mouth, and the wrinkles puckered the corners of his eyes in the old fashion.

'Well done, Winn,' he said. 'I'm glad you asked that, though I'm not quite sure that I know the answer. Or rather I have two answers, and either may be correct. In the first place his own statement may have been strictly true. Your Quadrangle at night is beautiful, so beautiful that it gives a fresh joy to the eyes each time they rest on it. Hargreaves has lived there all his life, he's a materialist and all that, and yet human beings are curiously compounded, and there's a love of beauty deep in the hearts of us all. Don't you think it's possible that as he stepped out into the Quadrangle that night he was struck afresh by its grace and calm so that he wanted to feast his eyes on it for a few minutes whilst the mood was on him? But there's another explanation, and I'm afraid it's more probable. Shirley had come in that night, ostensibly to talk about the Library. But very soon Hargreaves was to become his brother-in-law by marriage, and as such a member of his family. Shirley was a man who saw things clearly and he didn't mince his words. Don't you think it probable that Hargreaves wasn't quite easy in his conscience; that he was afraid that Shirley might have something to say about his manner of life and his doubtful pleasures? Don't you think, I mean, that Hargreaves was a little frightened of that interview, and that he was postponing it as long as he decently could? That, I'm afraid, is what I believe, though of course I can't tell. But there's one curious little fact about it. It was because Hargreaves *did* spend ten minutes outside before he came back to us that I ultimately decided in my mind that he must be innocent. Listen. He is whatever his shortcomings, a very able man, and if he had planned a murder he would have done it with the maximum of efficiency. Well, I put myself in his place. One morning, when no one was about, I went to Common Room and took out my watch. I walked thence to Hargreaves' rooms; I listened to see that no one was watching me; I opened the door, I lifted an imaginary revolver from the table and I shot an imaginary man. Then I turned on the lights to see that I had left no traces, and I felt the imaginary heart of the imaginary corpse. I walked back to the Common Room slowly and I looked at my watch again. I had taken just five and a half minutes over the whole proceeding. No, I said to myself, if Hargreaves had killed Shirley he would have wished to summon us as quickly as he could, for every minute increased his personal danger. He would have been back in Common Room within six minutes, and not after ten. At first I thought exactly the opposite of all this; I thought that he would have been afraid that we should notice that the murder had only that moment been committed, and he would have waited. But the more I pondered over it the more clearly I saw that the danger of delay would seem far more menacing to him than the danger of our too accurate observations. I felt convinced that if he had been the murderer he would have been back in Common Room in the shortest possible time. The little fact of his delay, which seemed so damning for him, was in my considered view his greatest safeguard.'

# CHAPTER EIGHTEEN

I T's the last Sunday of term, and I'm sitting alone in my
rooms. I ought to be at evening chapel, but I can't stand
Mitton's sermons; for one thing they're always the same –
he's telling them now that everything is for the best because
God is watching over all our doings. In a moment he'll be
talking of the 'trivial round, the common task' and working
up towards his peroration about hard work and simple
faith. I suppose it's all right, but I couldn't bear it to-night.

My mind keeps straying back over the days that have
passed since Mottram's suicide . . . I'm in the Coroner's
Court again, and listening to his solemn inanities. How
exactly they misrepresent the true facts! He's dwelling
unctuously now on the brilliant promise of the dead man,
he's speaking of the over-stretched bow which snaps suddenly, he's alluded with just the right touch of dignified
sympathy to the dead man's grief at Shirley's death and
his disappointment at his scientific setback . . . The verdict's
a foregone conclusion, of course, but he must say his words
. . . And now I'm saying farewell to Mary – she's going with
her sister for a long sea-voyage, to forget it all, but they
never will forget. She presses my hand and thanks me
'for all I've done,' but her eyes betray her, and tell me
the truth. She thinks that I have failed her. And of
Mottram she speaks with a cruelty, which is no less cruel
because it is quite unconscious. 'Oh, Mr Winn, I liked
him so much: I could never have believed that he would
be so weak and . . . yes, so wicked as to take his own life.'
My lips are sealed; I can't save his memory even from
that . . . Another farewell. I am standing on the platform
as Brendel's train moves out. He looks at me with a smile
of good-will, which is also, somehow, full of pity. I suppose
he knows that my life is all broken up. Shall I ever see

him again, I wonder, and gather strength from his encouragement? . . . I'm in Common Room, and they're still talking about the mystery of the murder. They'll never find out now. Hargreaves is no longer with us. He asked the college for a year's leave of absence, and we let him go. Somehow no one, not even the best of his friends, wanted him to stay. I don't think he'll ever come back. But the others are speaking of the murder as though it had happened a year ago. Really their minds are on other things – they're concerned with the future rather than the past. Shepardson is thinking of the changes he will make in the Library, where he has succeeded Shirley; Doyne is full of his new duties as Dean. How infernally callous they all are! Trower is much concerned to fill Hargreaves' rooms. 'Such a damned nuisance, Winn; no one wants to live where there's been a murder. But I've got a plan. I'm going to turn that set into a lecture room. Young men nowadays are always cutting lectures, but the thought of going to a room where a poor devil was done in may attract their curiosity. Yes. I'll turn that set into a lecture room. Rather a sound idea, what?' Curse the man; hasn't he any sensibility at all? . . .

In chapel they're just starting the last hymn, for I can hear the organ. Ah. It's just what Mitton would choose to-night!

*God moves in a mysterious way*
*His wonders to perform.*

A grand hymn and grand music, but it doesn't fit my mood. How can it, when everything has gone wrong! . . . Shirley and Mottram are dead, and Hargreaves will never come back, and Ruth and Mary are lost to me. My friends are all gone, and I'm lonely . . . I wonder if, with all their callousness, Doyne and Trower and Shepardson aren't really right? How little the life of a great college like this concerns itself with any individual, how easily it goes on without him! How much would any of them care if I went to-morrow? How long should I be remembered? The individual passes, but the college goes on ... But I can't bring myself into tune with new ideas. I can't help thinking only of the disastrous past. It's all wrong – all tragic, and life spells futility, and failure, and frustration ... They're getting to the end of that hymn now, and I can hear those tremendous last lines:

*God is His own interpreter,*
*And He will make it plain.*

If only I could really believe that; if only I had the sort of blind faith that Mitton has! But I *can't* believe it; it will never be plain to me ... Perhaps I am too old.

# A CATALOGUE OF
# SELECTED DOVER BOOKS
# IN ALL FIELDS OF INTEREST

# A CATALOGUE OF SELECTED DOVER
# BOOKS IN ALL FIELDS OF INTEREST

RACKHAM'S COLOR ILLUSTRATIONS FOR WAGNER'S RING. Rackham's finest mature work—all 64 full-color watercolors in a faithful and lush interpretation of the *Ring*. Full-sized plates on coated stock of the paintings used by opera companies for authentic staging of Wagner. Captions aid in following complete Ring cycle. Introduction. 64 illustrations plus vignettes. 72pp. 8⅝ x 11¼. 23779-6 Pa. $6.00

CONTEMPORARY POLISH POSTERS IN FULL COLOR, edited by Joseph Czestochowski. 46 full-color examples of brilliant school of Polish graphic design, selected from world's first museum (near Warsaw) dedicated to poster art. Posters on circuses, films, plays, concerts all show cosmopolitan influences, free imagination. Introduction. 48pp. 9⅜ x 12¼. 23780-X Pa. $6.00

GRAPHIC WORKS OF EDVARD MUNCH, Edvard Munch. 90 haunting, evocative prints by first major Expressionist artist and one of the greatest graphic artists of his time: *The Scream, Anxiety, Death Chamber, The Kiss, Madonna,* etc. Introduction by Alfred Werner. 90pp. 9 x 12. 23765-6 Pa. $5.00

THE GOLDEN AGE OF THE POSTER, Hayward and Blanche Cirker. 70 extraordinary posters in full colors, from Maitres de l'Affiche, Mucha, Lautrec, Bradley, Cheret, Beardsley, many others. Total of 78pp. 9⅜ x 12¼. 22753-7 Pa. $5.95

THE NOTEBOOKS OF LEONARDO DA VINCI, edited by J. P. Richter. Extracts from manuscripts reveal great genius; on painting, sculpture, anatomy, sciences, geography, etc. Both Italian and English. 186 ms. pages reproduced, plus 500 additional drawings, including studies for *Last Supper,* Sforza monument, etc. 860pp. 7⅞ x 10¾. (Available in U.S. only) 22572-0, 22573-9 Pa., Two-vol. set $15.90

THE CODEX NUTTALL, as first edited by Zelia Nuttall. Only inexpensive edition, in full color, of a pre-Columbian Mexican (Mixtec) book. 88 color plates show kings, gods, heroes, temples, sacrifices. New explanatory, historical introduction by Arthur G. Miller. 96pp. 11⅜ x 8½. (Available in U.S. only) 23168-2 Pa. $7.95

UNE SEMAINE DE BONTÉ, A SURREALISTIC NOVEL IN COLLAGE, Max Ernst. Masterpiece created out of 19th-century periodical illustrations, explores worlds of terror and surprise. Some consider this Ernst's greatest work. 208pp. 8⅛ x 11. 23252-2 Pa. $5.00

DRAWINGS OF WILLIAM BLAKE, William Blake. 92 plates from Book of Job, *Divine Comedy, Paradise Lost,* visionary heads, mythological figures, Laocoon, etc. Selection, introduction, commentary by Sir Geoffrey Keynes. 178pp. 8⅛ x 11.                    22303-5 Pa. $4.00

ENGRAVINGS OF HOGARTH, William Hogarth. 101 of Hogarth's greatest works: *Rake's Progress, Harlot's Progress, Illustrations for Hudibras, Before and After, Beer Street and Gin Lane,* many more. Full commentary. 256pp. 11 x 13¾.                    22479-1 Pa. $12.95

DAUMIER: 120 GREAT LITHOGRAPHS, Honore Daumier. Wide-ranging collection of lithographs by the greatest caricaturist of the 19th century. Concentrates on eternally popular series on lawyers, on married life, on liberated women, etc. Selection, introduction, and notes on plates by Charles F. Ramus. Total of 158pp. 9⅜ x 12¼.          23512-2 Pa. $5.50

DRAWINGS OF MUCHA, Alphonse Maria Mucha. Work reveals drafts-man of highest caliber: studies for famous posters and paintings, render-ings for book illustrations and ads, etc. 70 works, 9 in color; including 6 items not drawings. Introduction. List of illustrations. 72pp. 9⅜ x 12¼. (Available in U.S. only)                    23672-2 Pa. $4.00

GIOVANNI BATTISTA PIRANESI: DRAWINGS IN THE PIERPONT MORGAN LIBRARY, Giovanni Battista Piranesi. For first time ever all of Morgan Library's collection, world's largest. 167 illustrations of rare Piranesi drawings—archeological, architectural, decorative and visionary. Essay, detailed list of drawings, chronology, captions. Edited by Felice Stampfle. 144pp. 9⅜ x 12¼.                    23714-1 Pa. $7.50

NEW YORK ETCHINGS (1905-1949), John Sloan. All of important American artist's N.Y. life etchings. 67 works include some of his best art; also lively historical record—Greenwich Village, tenement scenes. Edited by Sloan's widow. Introduction and captions. 79pp. 8⅜ x 11¼.
                    23651-X Pa. $4.00

CHINESE PAINTING AND CALLIGRAPHY: A PICTORIAL SURVEY, Wan-go Weng. 69 fine examples from John M. Crawford's matchless private collection: landscapes, birds, flowers, human figures, etc., plus calligraphy. Every basic form included: hanging scrolls, handscrolls, album leaves, fans, etc. 109 illustrations. Introduction. Captions. 192pp. 8⅞ x 11¾.
                    23707-9 Pa. $7.95

DRAWINGS OF REMBRANDT, edited by Seymour Slive. Updated Lipp-mann, Hofstede de Groot edition, with definitive scholarly apparatus. All portraits, biblical sketches, landscapes, nudes, Oriental figures, classical studies, together with selection of work by followers. 550 illustrations. Total of 630pp. 9⅛ x 12¼.    21485-0, 21486-9 Pa., Two-vol. set $15.00

THE DISASTERS OF WAR, Francisco Goya. 83 etchings record horrors of Napoleonic wars in Spain and war in general. Reprint of 1st edition, plus 3 additional plates. Introduction by Philip Hofer. 97pp. 9⅜ x 8¼.
                    21872-4 Pa. $3.75

THE EARLY WORK OF AUBREY BEARDSLEY, Aubrey Beardsley. 157 plates, 2 in color: *Manon Lescaut, Madame Bovary, Morte Darthur, Salome,* other. Introduction by H. Marillier. 182pp. 8⅛ x 11. 21816-3 Pa. $4.50

THE LATER WORK OF AUBREY BEARDSLEY, Aubrey Beardsley. Exotic masterpieces of full maturity: *Venus and Tannhauser, Lysistrata, Rape of the Lock, Volpone,* Savoy material, etc. 174 plates, 2 in color. 186pp. 8⅛ x 11. 21817-1 Pa. $4.50

THOMAS NAST'S CHRISTMAS DRAWINGS, Thomas Nast. Almost all Christmas drawings by creator of image of Santa Claus as we know it, and one of America's foremost illustrators and political cartoonists. 66 illustrations. 3 illustrations in color on covers. 96pp. 8⅜ x 11¼. 23660-9 Pa. $3.50

THE DORÉ ILLUSTRATIONS FOR DANTE'S DIVINE COMEDY, Gustave Doré. All 135 plates from Inferno, Purgatory, Paradise; fantastic tortures, infernal landscapes, celestial wonders. Each plate with appropriate (translated) verses. 141pp. 9 x 12. 23231-X Pa. $4.50

DORÉ'S ILLUSTRATIONS FOR RABELAIS, Gustave Doré. 252 striking illustrations of *Gargantua and Pantagruel* books by foremost 19th-century illustrator. Including 60 plates, 192 delightful smaller illustrations. 153pp. 9 x 12. 23656-0 Pa. $5.00

LONDON: A PILGRIMAGE, Gustave Doré, Blanchard Jerrold. Squalor, riches, misery, beauty of mid-Victorian metropolis; 55 wonderful plates, 125 other illustrations, full social, cultural text by Jerrold. 191pp. of text. 9⅜ x 12¼. 22306-X Pa. $7.00

THE RIME OF THE ANCIENT MARINER, Gustave Doré, S. T. Coleridge. Dore's finest work, 34 plates capture moods, subtleties of poem. Full text. Introduction by Millicent Rose. 77pp. 9¼ x 12. 22305-1 Pa. $3.50

THE DORE BIBLE ILLUSTRATIONS, Gustave Doré. All wonderful, detailed plates: Adam and Eve, Flood, Babylon, Life of Jesus, etc. Brief King James text with each plate. Introduction by Millicent Rose. 241 plates. 241pp. 9 x 12. 23004-X Pa. $6.00

THE COMPLETE ENGRAVINGS, ETCHINGS AND DRYPOINTS OF ALBRECHT DURER. "Knight, Death and Devil"; "Melencolia," and more—all Dürer's known works in all three media, including 6 works formerly attributed to him. 120 plates. 235pp. 8⅜ x 11¼. 22851-7 Pa. $6.50

MAXIMILIAN'S TRIUMPHAL ARCH, Albrecht Dürer and others. Incredible monument of woodcut art: 8 foot high elaborate arch—heraldic figures, humans, battle scenes, fantastic elements—that you can assemble yourself. Printed on one side, layout for assembly. 143pp. 11 x 16. 21451-6 Pa. $5.00

THE COMPLETE WOODCUTS OF ALBRECHT DURER, edited by Dr. W. Kurth. 346 in all: "Old Testament," "St. Jerome," "Passion," "Life of Virgin," Apocalypse," many others. Introduction by Campbell Dodgson. 285pp. 8½ x 12¼.                21097-9 Pa. $7.50

DRAWINGS OF ALBRECHT DURER, edited by Heinrich Wolfflin. 81 plates show development from youth to full style. Many favorites; many new. Introduction by Alfred Werner. 96pp. 8⅛ x 11.   22352-3 Pa. $5.00

THE HUMAN FIGURE, Albrecht Dürer. Experiments in various techniques—stereometric, progressive proportional, and others. Also life studies that rank among finest ever done. Complete reprinting of *Dresden Sketchbook*. 170 plates. 355pp. 8⅜ x 11¼.            21042-1 Pa. $7.95

OF THE JUST SHAPING OF LETTERS, Albrecht Dürer. Renaissance artist explains design of Roman majuscules by geometry, also Gothic lower and capitals. Grolier Club edition. 43pp. 7⅞ x 10¾   21306-4 Pa. $3.00

TEN BOOKS ON ARCHITECTURE, Vitruvius. The most important book ever written on architecture. Early Roman aesthetics, technology, classical orders, site selection, all other aspects. Stands behind everything since. Morgan translation. 331pp. 5⅜ x 8½.         20645-9 Pa. $4.50

THE FOUR BOOKS OF ARCHITECTURE, Andrea Palladio. 16th-century classic responsible for Palladian movement and style. Covers classical architectural remains, Renaissance revivals, classical orders, etc. 1738 Ware English edition. Introduction by A. Placzek. 216 plates. 110pp. of text. 9½ x 12¾.                      21308-0 Pa. $10.00

HORIZONS, Norman Bel Geddes. Great industrialist stage designer, "father of streamlining," on application of aesthetics to transportation, amusement, architecture, etc. 1932 prophetic account; function, theory, specific projects. 222 illustrations. 312pp. 7⅞ x 10¾.             23514-9 Pa. $6.95

FRANK LLOYD WRIGHT'S FALLINGWATER, Donald Hoffmann. Full, illustrated story of conception and building of Wright's masterwork at Bear Run, Pa. 100 photographs of site, construction, and details of completed structure. 112pp. 9¼ x 10.               23671-4 Pa. **$5.50**

THE ELEMENTS OF DRAWING, John Ruskin. Timeless classic by great Viltorian; starts with basic ideas, works through more difficult. Many practical exercises. 48 illustrations. Introduction by Lawrence Campbell. 228pp. 5⅜ x 8½.                       22730-8 Pa. $3.75

GIST OF ART, John Sloan. Greatest modern American teacher, Art Students League, offers innumerable hints, instructions, guided comments to help you in painting. Not a formal course. 46 illustrations. Introduction by Helen Sloan. 200pp. 5⅜ x 8½.           23435-5 Pa. **$4.00**

THE ANATOMY OF THE HORSE, George Stubbs. Often considered the great masterpiece of animal anatomy. Full reproduction of 1766 edition, plus prospectus; original text and modernized text. 36 plates. Introduction by Eleanor Garvey. 121pp. 11 x 14¾.                                    23402-9 Pa. $6.00

BRIDGMAN'S LIFE DRAWING, George B. Bridgman. More than 500 illustrative drawings and text teach you to abstract the body into its major masses, use light and shade, proportion; as well as specific areas of anatomy, of which Bridgman is master. 192pp. 6½ x 9¼. (Available in U.S. only)
22710-3 Pa. $3.50

ART NOUVEAU DESIGNS IN COLOR, Alphonse Mucha, Maurice Verneuil, Georges Auriol. Full-color reproduction of *Combinaisons ornementales* (c. 1900) by Art Nouveau masters. Floral, animal, geometric, interlacings, swashes—borders, frames, spots—all incredibly beautiful. 60 plates, hundreds of designs. 9⅜ x 8-1/16.                           22885-1 Pa. $4.00

FULL-COLOR FLORAL DESIGNS IN THE ART NOUVEAU STYLE, E. A. Seguy. 166 motifs, on 40 plates, from *Les fleurs et leurs applications decoratives* (1902): borders, circular designs, repeats, allovers, "spots." All in authentic Art Nouveau colors. 48pp. 9⅜ x 12¼.
23439-8 Pa. $5.00

A DIDEROT PICTORIAL ENCYCLOPEDIA OF TRADES AND IN-DUSTRY, edited by Charles C. Gillispie. 485 most interesting plates from the great French Encyclopedia of the 18th century show hundreds of working figures, artifacts, process, land and cityscapes; glassmaking, paper-making, metal extraction, construction, weaving, making furniture, clothing, wigs, dozens of other activities. Plates fully explained. 920pp. 9 x 12.
22284-5, 22285-3 Clothbd., Two-vol. set $40.00

HANDBOOK OF EARLY ADVERTISING ART, Clarence P. Hornung. Largest collection of copyright-free early and antique advertising art ever compiled. Over 6,000 illustrations, from Franklin's time to the 1890's for special effects, novelty. Valuable source, almost inexhaustible.
Pictorial Volume. Agriculture, the zodiac, animals, autos, birds, Christmas, fire engines, flowers, trees, musical instruments, ships, games and sports, much more. Arranged by subject matter and use. 237 plates. 288pp. 9 x 12.
20122-8 Clothbd. $14..50

Typographical Volume. Roman and Gothic faces ranging from 10 point to 300 point, "Barnum," German and Old English faces, script, logotypes, scrolls and flourishes, 1115 ornamental initials, 67 complete alphabets, more. 310 plates. 320pp. 9 x 12.                           20123-6 Clothbd. $15.00

CALLIGRAPHY (CALLIGRAPHIA LATINA), J. G. Schwandner. High point of 18th-century ornamental calligraphy. Very ornate initials, scrolls, borders, cherubs, birds, lettered examples. 172pp. 9 x 13.
20475-8 Pa. $7.00

ART FORMS IN NATURE, Ernst Haeckel. Multitude of strangely beautiful natural forms: Radiolaria, Foraminifera, jellyfishes, fungi, turtles, bats, etc. All 100 plates of the 19th-century evolutionist's *Kunstformen der Natur* (1904). 100pp. 9⅜ x 12¼.                    22987-4 Pa. $5.00

CHILDREN: A PICTORIAL ARCHIVE FROM NINETEENTH-CENTURY SOURCES, edited by Carol Belanger Grafton. 242 rare, copyright-free wood engravings for artists and designers. Widest such selection available. All illustrations in line. 119pp. 8⅜ x 11¼.
23694-3 Pa. $3.50

WOMEN: A PICTORIAL ARCHIVE FROM NINETEENTH-CENTURY SOURCES, edited by Jim Harter. 391 copyright-free wood engravings for artists and designers selected from rare periodicals. Most extensive such collection available. All illustrations in line. 128pp. 9 x 12.
23703-6 Pa. $4.50

ARABIC ART IN COLOR, Prisse d'Avennes. From the greatest ornamentalists of all time—50 plates in color, rarely seen outside the Near East, rich in suggestion and stimulus. Includes 4 plates on covers. 46pp. 9⅜ x 12¼.                    23658-7 Pa. $6.00

AUTHENTIC ALGERIAN CARPET DESIGNS AND MOTIFS, edited by June Beveridge. Algerian carpets are world famous. Dozens of geometrical motifs are charted on grids, color-coded, for weavers, needleworkers, craftsmen, designers. 53 illustrations plus 4 in color. 48pp. 8¼ x 11. (Available in U.S. only)                    23650-1 Pa. $1.75

DICTIONARY OF AMERICAN PORTRAITS, edited by Hayward and Blanche Cirker. 4000 important Americans, earliest times to 1905, mostly in clear line. Politicians, writers, soldiers, scientists, inventors, industrialists, Indians, Blacks, women, outlaws, etc. Identificatory information. 756pp. 9¼ x 12¾.                    21823-6 Clothbd. $40.00

HOW THE OTHER HALF LIVES, Jacob A. Riis. Journalistic record of filth, degradation, upward drive in New York immigrant slums, shops, around 1900. New edition includes 100 original Riis photos, monuments of early photography. 233pp. 10 x 7⅞.                    22012-5 Pa. $7.00

NEW YORK IN THE THIRTIES, Berenice Abbott. Noted photographer's fascinating study of city shows new buildings that have become famous and old sights that have disappeared forever. Insightful commentary. 97 photographs. 97pp. 11⅜ x 10.                    22967-X Pa. $5.00

MEN AT WORK, Lewis W. Hine. Famous photographic studies of construction workers, railroad men, factory workers and coal miners. New supplement of 18 photos on Empire State building construction. New introduction by Jonathan L. Doherty. Total of 69 photos. 63pp. 8 x 10¾.
23475-4 Pa. $3.00

THE DEPRESSION YEARS AS PHOTOGRAPHED BY ARTHUR ROTH-
STEIN, Arthur Rothstein. First collection devoted entirely to the work of
outstanding 1930s photographer: famous dust storm photo, ragged children,
unemployed, etc. 120 photographs. Captions. 119pp. 9¼ x 10¾.
23590-4 Pa. $5.00

CAMERA WORK: A PICTORIAL GUIDE, Alfred Stieglitz. All 559 illustrations and plates from the most important periodical in the history of
art photography, Camera Work (1903-17). Presented four to a page, reduced in size but still clear, in strict chronological order, with complete
captions. Three indexes. Glossary. Bibliography. 176pp. 8⅜ x 11¼.
23591-2 Pa. $6.95

ALVIN LANGDON COBURN, PHOTOGRAPHER, Alvin L. Coburn. Revealing autobiography by one of greatest photographers of 20th century
gives insider's version of Photo-Secession, plus comments on his own work.
77 photographs by Coburn. Edited by Helmut and Alison Gernsheim.
160pp. 8⅛ x 11. 23685-4 Pa. $6.00

NEW YORK IN THE FORTIES, Andreas Feininger. 162 brilliant photographs by the well-known photographer, formerly with Life magazine, show
commuters, shoppers, Times Square at night, Harlem nightclub, Lower
East Side, etc. Introduction and full captions by John von Hartz. 181pp.
9¼ x 10¾. 23585-8 Pa. $6.00

GREAT NEWS PHOTOS AND THE STORIES BEHIND THEM, John
Faber. Dramatic volume of 140 great news photos, 1855 through 1976,
and revealing stories behind them, with both historical and technical information. Hindenburg disaster, shooting of Oswald, nomination of Jimmy
Carter, etc. 160pp. 8¼ x 11. 23667-6 Pa. $5.00

THE ART OF THE CINEMATOGRAPHER, Leonard Maltin. Survey of
American cinematography history and anecdotal interviews with 5 masters—
Arthur Miller, Hal Mohr, Hal Rosson, Lucien Ballard, and Conrad Hall.
Very large selection of behind-the-scenes production photos. 105 photo-
graphs. Filmographies. Index. Originally Behind the Camera. 144pp.
8¼ x 11. 23686-2 Pa. $5.00

DESIGNS FOR THE THREE-CORNERED HAT (LE TRICORNE),
Pablo Picasso. 32 fabulously rare drawings—including 31 color illustrations
of costumes and accessories—for 1919 production of famous ballet. Edited
by Parmenia Migel, who has written new introduction. 48pp. 9⅜ x 12¼.
(Available in U.S. only) 23709-5 Pa. $5.00

NOTES OF A FILM DIRECTOR, Sergei Eisenstein. Greatest Russian
filmmaker explains montage, making of Alexander Nevsky, aesthetics; comments on self, associates, great rivals (Chaplin), similar material. 78 illustrations. 240pp. 5⅜ x 8½. 22392-2 Pa. $4.50

HOLLYWOOD GLAMOUR PORTRAITS, edited by John Kobal. 145 photos capture the stars from 1926-49, the high point in portrait photography. Gable, Harlow, Bogart, Bacall, Hedy Lamarr, Marlene Dietrich, Robert Montgomery, Marlon Brando, Veronica Lake; 94 stars in all. Full background on photographers, technical aspects, much more. Total of 160pp. 8⅜ x 11¼.                                   23352-9 Pa. **$6.00**

THE NEW YORK STAGE: FAMOUS PRODUCTIONS IN PHOTOGRAPHS, edited by Stanley Appelbaum. 148 photographs from Museum of City of New York show 142 plays, 1883-1939. *Peter Pan, The Front Page, Dead End, Our Town,* O'Neill, hundreds of actors and actresses, etc. Full indexes. 154pp. 9½ x 10.                              23241-7 Pa. **$6.00**

DIALOGUES CONCERNING TWO NEW SCIENCES, Galileo Galilei. Encompassing 30 years of experiment and thought, these dialogues deal with geometric demonstrations of fracture of solid bodies, cohesion, leverage, speed of light and sound, pendulums, falling bodies, accelerated motion, etc. 300pp. 5⅜ x 8½.                           60099-8 Pa. $4.00

THE GREAT OPERA STARS IN HISTORIC PHOTOGRAPHS, edited by James Camner. 343 portraits from the 1850s to the 1940s: Tamburini, Mario, Caliapin, Jeritza, Melchior, Melba, Patti, Pinza, Schipa, Caruso, Farrar, Steber, Gobbi, and many more—270 performers in all. Index. 199pp. 8⅜ x 11¼.                                 23575-0 Pa. $6.50

J. S. BACH, Albert Schweitzer. Great full-length study of Bach, life, background to music, music, by foremost modern scholar. Ernest Newman translation. 650 musical examples. Total of 928pp. 5⅜ x 8½. (Available in U.S. only)          21631-4, 21632-2 Pa., Two-vol. set $11.00

COMPLETE PIANO SONATAS, Ludwig van Beethoven. All sonatas in the fine Schenker edition, with fingering, analytical material. One of best modern editions. Total of 615pp. 9 x 12. (Available in U.S. only)
                              23134-8, 23135-6 Pa., Two-vol. set $15.00

KEYBOARD MUSIC, J. S. Bach. Bach-Gesellschaft edition. For harpsichord, piano, other keyboard instruments. English Suites, French Suites, Six Partitas, Goldberg Variations, Two-Part Inventions, Three-Part Sinfonias. 312pp. 8⅛ x 11. (Available in U.S. only)      22360-4 Pa. **$6.95**

FOUR SYMPHONIES IN FULL SCORE, Franz Schubert. Schubert's four most popular symphonies: No. 4 in C Minor ("Tragic"); No. 5 in B-flat Major; No. 8 in B Minor ("Unfinished"); No. 9 in C Major ("Great"). Breitkopf & Hartel edition. Study score. 261pp. 9⅜ x 12¼.
                                                 23681-1 Pa. $6.50

THE AUTHENTIC GILBERT & SULLIVAN SONGBOOK, W. S. Gilbert, A. S. Sullivan. Largest selection available; 92 songs, uncut, original keys, in piano rendering approved by Sullivan. Favorites and lesser-known fine numbers. Edited with plot synopses by James Spero. 3 illustrations. 399pp. 9 x 12.                                          23482-7 Pa. $9.95

PRINCIPLES OF ORCHESTRATION, Nikolay Rimsky-Korsakov. Great classical orchestrator provides fundamentals of tonal resonance, progression of parts, voice and orchestra, tutti effects, much else in major document. 330pp. of musical excerpts. 489pp. 6½ x 9¼. 21266-1 Pa. $7.50

TRISTAN UND ISOLDE, Richard Wagner. Full orchestral score with complete instrumentation. Do not confuse with piano reduction. Commentary by Felix Mottl, great Wagnerian conductor and scholar. Study score. 655pp. 8⅛ x 11. 22915-7 Pa. $13.95

REQUIEM IN FULL SCORE, Giuseppe Verdi. Immensely popular with choral groups and music lovers. Republication of edition published by C. F. Peters, Leipzig, n. d. German frontmaker in English translation. Glossary. Text in Latin. Study score. 204pp. 9⅜ x 12¼.
23682-X Pa. $6.00

COMPLETE CHAMBER MUSIC FOR STRINGS, Felix Mendelssohn. All of Mendelssohn's chamber music: Octet, 2 Quintets, 6 Quartets, and Four Pieces for String Quartet. (Nothing with piano is included). Complete works edition (1874-7). Study score. 283 pp. 9⅜ x 12¼.
23679-X Pa. $7.50

POPULAR SONGS OF NINETEENTH-CENTURY AMERICA, edited by Richard Jackson. 64 most important songs: "Old Oaken Bucket," "Arkansas Traveler," "Yellow Rose of Texas," etc. Authentic original sheet music, full introduction and commentaries. 290pp. 9 x 12. 23270-0 Pa. $7.95

COLLECTED PIANO WORKS, Scott Joplin. Edited by Vera Brodsky Lawrence. Practically all of Joplin's piano works—rags, two-steps, marches, waltzes, etc., 51 works in all. Extensive introduction by Rudi Blesh. Total of 345pp. 9 x 12. 23106-2 Pa. $14.95

BASIC PRINCIPLES OF CLASSICAL BALLET, Agrippina Vaganova. Great Russian theoretician, teacher explains methods for teaching classical ballet; incorporates best from French, Italian, Russian schools. 118 illustrations. 175pp. 5⅜ x 8½. 22036-2 Pa. $2.50

CHINESE CHARACTERS, L. Wieger. Rich analysis of 2300 characters according to traditional systems into primitives. Historical-semantic analysis to phonetics (Classical Mandarin) and radicals. 820pp. 6⅛ x 9¼.
21321-8 Pa. $10.00

EGYPTIAN LANGUAGE: EASY LESSONS IN EGYPTIAN HIERO-GLYPHICS, E. A. Wallis Budge. Foremost Egyptologist offers Egyptian grammar, explanation of hieroglyphics, many reading texts, dictionary of symbols. 246pp. 5 x 7½. (Available in U.S. only)
21394-3 Clothbd. $7.50

AN ETYMOLOGICAL DICTIONARY OF MODERN ENGLISH, Ernest Weekley. Richest, fullest work, by foremost British lexicographer. Detailed word histories. Inexhaustible. Do not confuse this with Concise Etymological Dictionary, which is abridged. Total of 856pp. 6½ x 9¼.
21873-2, 21874-0 Pa., Two-vol. set $12.00

A MAYA GRAMMAR, Alfred M. Tozzer. Practical, useful English-language grammar by the Harvard anthropologist who was one of the three greatest American scholars in the area of Maya culture. Phonetics, grammatical processes, syntax, more. 301pp. 5⅜ x 8½.                23465-7 Pa. $4.00

THE JOURNAL OF HENRY D. THOREAU, edited by Bradford Torrey, F. H. Allen. Complete reprinting of 14 volumes, 1837-61, over two million words; the sourcebooks for *Walden*, etc. Definitive. All original sketches, plus 75 photographs. Introduction by Walter Harding. Total of 1804pp. 8½ x 12¼.                20312-3, 20313-1 Clothbd., Two-vol. set $50.00

CLASSIC GHOST STORIES, Charles Dickens and others. 18 wonderful stories you've wanted to reread: "The Monkey's Paw," "The House and the Brain," "The Upper Berth," "The Signalman," "Dracula's Guest," "The Tapestried Chamber," etc. Dickens, Scott, Mary Shelley, Stoker, etc. 330pp. 5⅜ x 8½.                20735-8 Pa. $4.50

SEVEN SCIENCE FICTION NOVELS, H. G. Wells. Full novels. *First Men in the Moon, Island of Dr. Moreau, War of the Worlds, Food of the Gods, Invisible Man, Time Machine, In the Days of the Comet.* A basic science-fiction library. 1015pp. 5⅜ x 8½. (Available in U.S. only)
                20264-X Clothbd. $8.95

ARMADALE, Wilkie Collins. Third great mystery novel by the author of *The Woman in White* and *The Moonstone.* Ingeniously plotted narrative shows an exceptional command of character, incident and mood. Original magazine version with 40 illustrations. 597pp. 5⅜ x 8½.
                23429-0 Pa. $6.00

MASTERS OF MYSTERY, H. Douglas Thomson. The first book in English (1931) devoted to history and aesthetics of detective story. Poe, Doyle, LeFanu, Dickens, many others, up to 1930. New introduction and notes by E. F. Bleiler. 288pp. 5⅜ x 8½. (Available in U.S. only)
                23606-4 Pa. $4.00

FLATLAND, E. A. Abbott. Science-fiction classic explores life of 2-D being in 3-D world. Read also as introduction to thought about hyperspace. Introduction by Banesh Hoffmann. 16 illustrations. 103pp. 5⅜ x 8½.
                20001-9 Pa. $2.00

THREE SUPERNATURAL NOVELS OF THE VICTORIAN PERIOD, edited, with an introduction, by E. F. Bleiler. Reprinted complete and unabridged, three great classics of the supernatural: *The Haunted Hotel* by Wilkie Collins, *The Haunted House at Latchford* by Mrs. J. H. Riddell, and *The Lost Stradivarius* by J. Meade Falkner. 325pp. 5⅜ x 8½.
                22571-2 Pa. $4.00

AYESHA: THE RETURN OF "SHE," H. Rider Haggard. Virtuoso sequel featuring the great mythic creation, Ayesha, in an adventure that is fully as good as the first book, *She.* Original magazine version, with 47 original illustrations by Maurice Greiffenhagen. 189pp. 6½ x 9¼.
                23649-8 Pa. $3.50

UNCLE SILAS, J. Sheridan LeFanu. Victorian Gothic mystery novel, considered by many best of period, even better than Collins or Dickens. Wonderful psychological terror. Introduction by Frederick Shroyer. 436pp. 5⅜ x 8½. 21715-9 Pa. $6.00

JURGEN, James Branch Cabell. The great erotic fantasy of the 1920's that delighted thousands, shocked thousands more. Full final text, Lane edition with 13 plates by Frank Pape. 346pp. 5⅜ x 8½. 23507-6 Pa. $4.50

THE CLAVERINGS, Anthony Trollope. Major novel, chronicling aspects of British Victorian society, personalities. Reprint of Cornhill serialization, 16 plates by M. Edwards; first reprint of full text. Introduction by Norman Donaldson. 412pp. 5⅜ x 8½. 23464-9 Pa. $5.00

KEPT IN THE DARK, Anthony Trollope. Unusual short novel about Victorian morality and abnormal psychology by the great English author. Probably the first American publication. Frontispiece by Sir John Millais. 92pp. 6½ x 9¼. 23609-9 Pa. $2.50

RALPH THE HEIR, Anthony Trollope. Forgotten tale of illegitimacy, inheritance. Master novel of Trollope's later years. Victorian country estates, clubs, Parliament, fox hunting, world of fully realized characters. Reprint of 1871 edition. 12 illustrations by F. A. Faser. 434pp. of text. 5⅜ x 8½. 23642-0 Pa. $5.00

YEKL and THE IMPORTED BRIDEGROOM AND OTHER STORIES OF THE NEW YORK GHETTO, Abraham Cahan. Film *Hester Street* based on *Yekl* (1896). Novel, other stories among first about Jewish immigrants of N.Y.'s East Side. Highly praised by W. D. Howells—Cahan "a new star of realism." New introduction by Bernard G. Richards. 240pp. 5⅜ x 8½. 22427-9 Pa. $3.50

THE HIGH PLACE, James Branch Cabell. Great fantasy writer's enchanting comedy of disenchantment set in 18th-century France. Considered by some critics to be even better than his famous *Jurgen*. 10 illustrations and numerous vignettes by noted fantasy artist Frank C. Pape. 320pp. 5⅜ x 8½. 23670-6 Pa. $4.00

ALICE'S ADVENTURES UNDER GROUND, Lewis Carroll. Facsimile of ms. Carroll gave Alice Liddell in 1864. Different in many ways from final Alice. Handlettered, illustrated by Carroll. Introduction by Martin Gardner. 128pp. 5⅜ x 8½. 21482-6 Pa. $2.00

FAVORITE ANDREW LANG FAIRY TALE BOOKS IN MANY COLORS, Andrew Lang. The four Lang favorites in a boxed set—the complete *Red, Green, Yellow* and *Blue* Fairy Books. 164 stories; 439 illustrations by Lancelot Speed, Henry Ford and G. P. Jacomb Hood. Total of about 1500pp. 5⅜ x 8½. 23407-X Boxed set, Pa. $14.95

HOUSEHOLD STORIES BY THE BROTHERS GRIMM. All the great Grimm stories: "Rumpelstiltskin," "Snow White," "Hansel and Gretel," etc., with 114 illustrations by Walter Crane. 269pp. 5⅜ x 8½.
21080-4 Pa. $3.50

SLEEPING BEAUTY, illustrated by Arthur Rackham. Perhaps the fullest, most delightful version ever, told by C. S. Evans. Rackham's best work. 49 illustrations. 110pp. 7⅞ x 10¾.
22756-1 Pa. $2.50

AMERICAN FAIRY TALES, L. Frank Baum. Young cowboy lassoes Father Time; dummy in Mr. Floman's department store window comes to life; and 10 other fairy tales. 41 illustrations by N. P. Hall, Harry Kennedy, Ike Morgan, and Ralph Gardner. 209pp. 5⅜ x 8½.
23643-9 Pa. $3.00

THE WONDERFUL WIZARD OF OZ, L. Frank Baum. Facsimile in full color of America's finest children's classic. Introduction by Martin Gardner. 143 illustrations by W. W. Denslow. 267pp. 5⅜ x 8½.
20691-2 Pa. $3.50

THE TALE OF PETER RABBIT, Beatrix Potter. The inimitable Peter's terrifying adventure in Mr. McGregor's garden, with all 27 wonderful, full-color Potter illustrations. 55pp. 4¼ x 5½. (Available in U.S. only)
22827-4 Pa. $1.25

THE STORY OF KING ARTHUR AND HIS KNIGHTS, Howard Pyle. Finest children's version of life of King Arthur. 48 illustrations by Pyle. 131pp. 6⅛ x 9¼.
21445-1 Pa. $4.95

CARUSO'S CARICATURES, Enrico Caruso. Great tenor's remarkable caricatures of self, fellow musicians, composers, others. Toscanini, Puccini, Farrar, etc. Impish, cutting, insightful. 473 illustrations. Preface by M. Sisca. 217pp. 8⅜ x 11¼.
23528-9 Pa. $6.95

PERSONAL NARRATIVE OF A PILGRIMAGE TO ALMADINAH AND MECCAH, Richard Burton. Great travel classic by remarkably colorful personality. Burton, disguised as a Moroccan, visited sacred shrines of Islam, narrowly escaping death. Wonderful observations of Islamic life, customs, personalities. 47 illustrations. Total of 959pp. 5⅜ x 8½.
21217-3, 21218-1 Pa., Two-vol. set $12.00

INCIDENTS OF TRAVEL IN YUCATAN, John L. Stephens. Classic (1843) exploration of jungles of Yucatan, looking for evidences of Maya civilization. Travel adventures, Mexican and Indian culture, etc. Total of 669pp. 5⅜ x 8½.
20926-1, 20927-X Pa., Two-vol. set $7.90

AMERICAN LITERARY AUTOGRAPHS FROM WASHINGTON IRVING TO HENRY JAMES, Herbert Cahoon, et al. Letters, poems, manuscripts of Hawthorne, Thoreau, Twain, Alcott, Whitman, 67 other prominent American authors. Reproductions, full transcripts and commentary. Plus checklist of all American Literary Autographs in The Pierpont Morgan Library. Printed on exceptionally high-quality paper. 136 illustrations. 212pp. 9⅛ x 12¼.
23548-3 Pa. $12.50

AN AUTOBIOGRAPHY, Margaret Sanger. Exciting personal account of hard-fought battle for woman's right to birth control, against prejudice, church, law. Foremost feminist document. 504pp. 5⅜ x 8½.
20470-7 Pa. $5.50

MY BONDAGE AND MY FREEDOM, Frederick Douglass. Born as a slave, Douglass became outspoken force in antislavery movement. The best of Douglass's autobiographies. Graphic description of slave life. Introduction by P. Foner. 464pp. 5⅜ x 8½. 22457-0 Pa. $5.50

LIVING MY LIFE, Emma Goldman. Candid, no holds barred account by foremost American anarchist: her own life, anarchist movement, famous contemporaries, ideas and their impact. Struggles and confrontations in America, plus deportation to U.S.S.R. Shocking inside account of persecution of anarchists under Lenin. 13 plates. Total of 944pp. 5⅜ x 8½.
22543-7, 22544-5 Pa., Two-vol. set $12.00

LETTERS AND NOTES ON THE MANNERS, CUSTOMS AND CONDITIONS OF THE NORTH AMERICAN INDIANS, George Catlin. Classic account of life among Plains Indians: ceremonies, hunt, warfare, etc. Dover edition reproduces for first time all original paintings. 312 plates. 572pp. of text. 6⅛ x 9¼. 22118-0, 22119-9 Pa.. Two-vol. set $12.00

THE MAYA AND THEIR NEIGHBORS, edited by Clarence L. Hay, others. Synoptic view of Maya civilization in broadest sense, together with Northern, Southern neighbors. Integrates much background, valuable detail not elsewhere. Prepared by greatest scholars: Kroeber, Morley, Thompson, Spinden, Vaillant, many others. Sometimes called Tozzer Memorial Volume. 60 illustrations, linguistic map. 634pp. 5⅜ x 8½.
23510-6 Pa. $7.50

HANDBOOK OF THE INDIANS OF CALIFORNIA, A. L. Kroeber. Foremost American anthropologist offers complete ethnographic study of each group. Monumental classic. 459 illustrations, maps. 995pp. 5⅜ x 8½.
23368-5 Pa. $13.00

SHAKTI AND SHAKTA, Arthur Avalon. First book to give clear, cohesive analysis of Shakta doctrine, Shakta ritual and Kundalini Shakti (yoga). Important work by one of world's foremost students of Shaktic and Tantric thought. 732pp. 5⅜ x 8½. (Available in U.S. only)
23645-5 Pa. $7.95

AN INTRODUCTION TO THE STUDY OF THE MAYA HIEROGLYPHS, Syvanus Griswold Morley. Classic study by one of the truly great figures in hieroglyph research. Still the best introduction for the student for reading Maya hieroglyphs. New introduction by J. Eric S. Thompson. 117 illustrations. 284pp. 5⅜ x 8½. 23108-9 Pa. $4.00

A STUDY OF MAYA ART, Herbert J. Spinden. Landmark classic interprets Maya symbolism, estimates styles, covers ceramics, architecture, murals, stone carvings as artforms. Still a basic book in area. New introduction by J. Eric Thompson. Over 750 illustrations. 341pp. 8⅜ x 11¼.
21235-1 Pa. $6.95

GEOMETRY, RELATIVITY AND THE FOURTH DIMENSION, Rudolf Rucker. Exposition of fourth dimension, means of visualization, concepts of relativity as Flatland characters continue adventures. Popular, easily followed yet accurate, profound. 141 illustrations. 133pp. 5⅜ x 8½.
23400-2 Pa. $2.75

THE ORIGIN OF LIFE, A. I. Oparin. Modern classic in biochemistry, the first rigorous examination of possible evolution of life from nitrocarbon compounds. Non-technical, easily followed. Total of 295pp. 5⅜ x 8½.
60213-3 Pa. $4.00

PLANETS, STARS AND GALAXIES, A. E. Fanning. Comprehensive introductory survey: the sun, solar system, stars, galaxies, universe, cosmology; quasars, radio stars, etc. 24pp. of photographs. 189pp. 5⅜ x 8½. (Available in U.S. only)
21680-2 Pa. $3.75

THE THIRTEEN BOOKS OF EUCLID'S ELEMENTS, translated with introduction and commentary by Sir Thomas L. Heath. Definitive edition. Textual and linguistic notes, mathematical analysis, 2500 years of critical commentary. Do not confuse with abridged school editions. Total of 1414pp. 5⅜ x 8½.
60088-2, 60089-0, 60090-4 Pa., Three-vol. set $18.50

*Prices subject to change without notice.*

Available at your book dealer or write for free catalogue to Dept. GI, Dover Publications, Inc., 180 Varick St., N.Y., N.Y. 10014. Dover publishes more than 175 books each year on science, elementary and advanced mathematics, biology, music, art, literary history, social sciences and other areas.